MARSHAL OF THE
BARREN PLAINS

When Marshal Rattigan Fletcher failed to stop Jasper Minx raiding the Ash Valley bank, he and his deputy Callan McBride were forced to leave in disgrace. In the town of Redemption, the pair are hired to find out why men from the Bleak Point silver mine have been disappearing — and when they discover that Jasper works there, they don't have to look far for a culprit. But as the miners side with Jasper, Rattigan will need all his instincts as a lawman if he is to bring his nemesis to justice . . .

I. J. PARNHAM

◆

MARSHAL OF THE BARREN PLAINS

Complete and Unabridged

LINFORD
Leicester

First published in Great Britain in 2017 by
Robert Hale
an imprint of The Crowood Press
Wiltshire

First Linford Edition
published 2019
by arrangement with
The Crowood Press
Wiltshire

A catalogue record for this book is available
from the British Library.

ISBN 978–1–4448–4275–3

Published by
F. A. Thorpe (Publishing)
Anstey, Leicestershire

Set by Words & Graphics Ltd.
Anstey, Leicestershire
Printed and bound in Great Britain by
T. J. International Ltd., Padstow, Cornwall

This book is printed on acid-free paper

Prologue

'We need to head back,' Jefford Clancy said. 'The supply wagon won't be arriving today.'

Woodrow Albright nodded. 'I guess you're right, but it'll be light for a while longer. We can wait for a few more minutes.'

Jefford and Woodrow were sitting on a rock a quarter-mile away from the entrance to the Bleak Point silver mine. This position afforded them an uninterrupted view across the Barren Plains, and if the wagon was approaching they would be able to see it even if it was many miles away.

'Why are you so eager to see it?' Jefford asked after they'd sat for another fifteen minutes. 'Even if it's another two weeks late, we won't go hungry.'

'I know.' Woodrow shrugged. 'But sitting here is something to do.'

Jefford noted Woodrow's hesitant tone that suggested there was a reason why he had come out here for the last two evenings. He didn't press the matter, accepting Woodrow's answer.

They were part of the team that fed the miners, and with the evening meal served this was one of the few breaks in their duties that they could enjoy. Aside from drinking and gambling they had little to occupy that time.

The mine was situated in the inhospitable terrain of the Barren Plains with the nearest settlement of Redemption being a gruelling eight-day journey away. Only the most determined and resilient, and in many people's view, the most foolhardy, worked here and the difficult journey ensured that they were isolated.

Woodrow was showing every sign of staying here until it was too dark to see the wagon even if it was out there; still, Jefford glanced around. Then he saw something that made him do a double take.

A man was standing beside a rock out on the plains. He was about a quarter-mile away and facing Bleak Point, his form providing only a silhouette against the lighter ground beyond.

'What do you make of that?' Jefford asked.

Woodrow was still peering ahead and Jefford had to repeat his question and then nudge his arm before he replied.

'Make of what?' Woodrow said. He looked to where Jefford was pointing but his expression didn't change.

'The man standing out . . . ' Jefford trailed off when he noticed that while he'd been attracting Woodrow's attention the man had disappeared. The ground surrounding the rock was mainly flat and so the man must have crouched down behind it.

'Are you saying you saw someone out there?' Woodrow said levelly.

Jefford turned back to him. 'I did, and now he's no longer there. I'm guessing from your calm expression that you're not surprised.'

Woodrow tipped back his hat and sighed.

'Three nights ago I saw a man standing out on the plains. That's why I wanted to come here, and this time with someone who could confirm that I wasn't seeing things.' Woodrow smiled. 'So I'm relieved you saw him, too.'

Jefford stood up. 'In that case, come on. He must be hiding behind that rock and we can find out who he is and what he's doing.'

Woodrow stayed sitting and shook his head.

'That won't do you no good. The first time I saw him I approached him, but by the time I reached the rock he was no longer there. I didn't catch sight of him again.'

Jefford surveyed the nearby terrain that, even in the last few minutes, had darkened noticeably. By the time they reached the rock they would be struggling to keep their footing on the stony ground, and the journey back to Bleak Point would be even harder.

'Then we'll head back to the mine and ask around,' he suggested. 'Somebody will know who he is.'

'You can try, but I guess you'll get the same reaction that I got.' Woodrow stood up and with a last glance at the rock, he turned towards the mine. 'They'll reckon you've lost your mind.'

'There's no reason for anyone to think that,' Jefford said as they made their way back to the entrance.

'There is.' Woodrow gulped and then stopped. 'That first time I got fairly close to him before he disappeared, and I saw enough for me to recognize him if I ever saw him again. So I mentioned the description to a few people and they all came up with the same name.'

Jefford turned to Woodrow and waited, but when he didn't continue Jefford gave a smile and a prompt.

'Who?' he said.

'Apparently, he looks like Larry Walker.'

Jefford winced. 'Larry Walker is dead.'

'I know,' Woodrow said.

1

'Trouble,' Callan McBride said, nudging Rattigan Fletcher in the ribs.

Rattigan turned and leaned back against the bar to see what had concerned him. He winced when he saw that Vick Johansson along with two of his colleagues, Eustace and Dempster, had just walked into the Sagebrush saloon, the biggest and most popular saloon in Redemption.

Yesterday, Vick and his colleagues had arrived in town after completing the long journey from the Bleak Point silver mine. They had grown tired of being miners, so they'd looked for work in a mercantile, but they'd been in a sour frame of mind and they'd got into a heated argument with the owners.

Then they'd moved on to the saloon where they'd drunk too much liquor, putting them in a fighting mood. So

Rattigan had thrown them out of the saloon with a warning not to come back unless they were prepared to be more sociable.

Although customers weren't allowed in the saloon if they were packing guns, the men's surly glares as they looked around the saloon room suggested that this afternoon they were still intent on carrying on where they'd left off yesterday.

Vick noticed a poker game in the corner. He nodded to Eustace and Dempster and they set off across the saloon room.

Four men were at the table, where two of them had locked horns over the latest hand. The stakes must have grown high as several customers had gravitated towards the table to watch proceedings. So it was that Rattigan and Callan were the only people who paid attention to the newcomers.

As one of the players was Benjamin Graham, the co-owner of the mercantile where the new arrivals had had an argument yesterday, the potential for trouble was obvious. Rattigan directed Callan to move closer to the poker table while he looked to the door.

The owner of the saloon had employed Rattigan and Callan to keep the peace here; the other member of their team, Schneider Wilson, was standing guard outside. As Schneider wasn't visible over the batwings, Rattigan headed to the door and slipped outside.

Schneider was standing on the boardwalk and looking into town, even though few people were out and about. Rattigan tapped an insistent foot on the boardwalk, but as that still failed to attract Schneider's attention he walked up to him.

'Why did you let Vick in?' he asked.

Schneider flinched, as if he hadn't been aware of his presence, then turned.

'Vick said that he's not here to cause trouble,' Schneider said while not meeting Rattigan's eye. 'And I reckon every man deserves a second chance.'

'You're right.' Rattigan waited until Schneider smiled and then slapped a hand on his shoulder. 'But that wasn't your decision to make. You should have checked with me first.'

Then he bundled Schneider along towards the door. Schneider thrust out a leg and stopped himself.

'I don't have to check every decision with you,' he said, swinging round to glare at Rattigan.

'Except you do, if you want to continue working here.' Rattigan glared at Schneider, but then softened his expression. 'And right now there's trouble brewing in the saloon and it's our job to deal with it.'

Despite this reminder of their duties, Schneider still stood for several moments before, with a shrug of his jacket, he moved on at his own pace.

Rattigan followed him, to find, when the two men slipped back into the saloon, that the situation was developing in the way Rattigan had feared.

Vick was standing to the side of the poker table with Eustace and Dempster flanking him. He was glaring at Benjamin, who had hunched his shoulders so that he could stare at his cards in an obvious attempt to ignore him.

Callan was standing on the other side of the table facing Vick, but he was doing nothing to inflame the situation. With a slow turn of his head Benjamin looked up at Vick.

'I've got nothing more to say to you,' he said.

Then he shooed Vick away and returned to considering his cards. His action made Vick snarl and then bat the cards from Benjamin's hand, sending them fluttering away.

With a scraping of chairs Benjamin and his opponent leapt to their feet to confront Vick, but Rattigan had already seen enough.

'Step away from the table, Vick,' he said. 'You didn't listen to my warning last night and now you're no longer welcome in here.'

11

'I'm not going nowhere until you change your mind,' Vick said. He squared up to Benjamin.

'Interrupting our game sure isn't making me feel that I made the wrong decision,' Benjamin said, gesturing at the strewn cards. 'You're not the kind of men I want working for me.'

'You're wrong. We're the kind of men that could give you a whole heap of — '

Vick didn't get to complete his threat as Benjamin snarled with anger and pushed him back for a pace. Vick righted himself and moved to repay Benjamin in kind, but before he could act Rattigan reached the table and stepped between them.

'You just don't seem to listen to sense, Vick,' he said. 'Back down now while you can still walk out of here.'

Vick sneered and swung a fist at Rattigan's jaw, but Rattigan raised an arm and blocked the intended blow. Then he grabbed Vick's wrist and twisted it while stepping to the side.

A moment later he was standing

behind Vick and holding him in an armlock. Then he shoved him forward until he bellied up to the table. Callan stepped up to Eustace and Dempster and directed a warning shake of the head at them, but they ignored the opportunity to back down.

Dempster launched a scything blow at Callan's face. Callan ducked beneath Dempster's swinging arm. When he came up he delivered a low punch into his opponent's stomach that made Dempster double over.

Eustace raised a fist, so Callan grabbed Dempster around the shoulders and with a firm shove he pushed him towards the other man. The two men collided and they both went down. By the time they'd disentangled themselves Callan was standing over them.

'You should stop causing trouble in here,' he said. 'You're not very good at it.'

His comment raised a laugh from the watching customers and, as if accepting that these men could be bested easily,

13

several other men moved in on them.

Vick muttered an oath and tried to shake Rattigan off, but that only encouraged Rattigan to push his head down to the table and hold him doubled over.

'Like Callan said,' Rattigan muttered in Vick's ear, 'you men aren't impressive. I reckon it's time for you to move on.'

'You'll pay for this,' Vick said. 'You'll all pay for this.'

Vick gave one last determined shake, but when that failed to dislodge Rattigan he sighed and relaxed.

Judging that the situation was now under control Rattigan nodded to Callan. Then he looked for Schneider who, in an untypical lack of reaction, hadn't got involved in the skirmish.

Instead, he was standing back from the table and keeping a cautious eye on everyone. With quick gestures Rattigan ordered Schneider and Callan to take custody of Eustace and Dempster.

While they secured their prisoners

and marched them on to the door, he turned to Benjamin.

'Do you want me to call for Marshal Hague?' he said.

'No,' Benjamin said. 'I can trust you to deal with these no-account varmints. The only thing that concerns me about this situation is that we didn't get to complete our showdown.'

When the other poker player grunted that he agreed Rattigan raised Vick's head to stand him upright. He was turning him to the door when Benjamin winced, then, a moment later a thud sounded behind him.

While still holding Vick from behind, Rattigan turned to find that Eustace had torn himself free from Schneider's clutches, leaving Schneider lying on his back on the floor. Callan was pushing Dempster aside while reaching for his gun; the reason became apparent when Eustace raised his hand, displaying a six-shooter that he must have concealed previously.

In a moment Eustace aimed the gun

at Benjamin. Without warning he fired. From the corner of his eye Rattigan saw Benjamin clutch his chest and drop to his knees.

While keeping his left hand on Vick's wrist, Rattigan threw his right hand to his holster. In response Vick attempted to tear himself free. Rattigan had to struggle to aim at Eustace, giving the gunman time to blast off two more shots.

Then Callan fired, his shot hitting Eustace in the side. Eustace arched his back before keeling over but, even before he'd hit the floor, Callan was turning to Dempster, who was slipping his hand into his jacket.

Before Dempster could withdraw his concealed weapon Callan fired a warning shot that winged his upper arm, making him cry out. He staggered a pace to the side, doubled over, while clutching his wounded arm. Then Callan swirled back to train his gun on Vick. Rattigan matched his action and thrust his gun into Vick's side.

Vick tensed, then he glanced down at Benjamin, who was lying still on the floor. He uttered a low chuckle.

'It seems Benjamin got what he deserved,' he said with delight.

'And now you'll be the one who'll pay for that.'

Vick shrugged. 'I did nothing wrong. Eustace did all the shooting.'

Rattigan swung Vick round and pressed him up against the table. He frisked him, but Vick didn't have a gun on him.

While Schneider took the wounded Dempster prisoner, Callan hurried over to Benjamin. He shook his head and moved on.

Two other poker players had been shot and Callan's worried expression suggested they were in a bad way, too.

'This sure is a mess,' he said as he stood up. 'We'll have no choice now but to hand this one over to Marshal Hague.'

Rattigan nodded. 'And if I were him, I wouldn't be happy about this.'

2

'You do believe our version of events, don't you?' Rattigan said when Marshal Hague returned to the law office.

'I've spoken with the customers in the saloon,' Hague said. He walked over to the stove and poured himself a coffee. 'The events are clear, but that doesn't excuse what you did.'

It was now approaching sundown; Rattigan and his men had been in the law office since the incident.

Vick and the wounded Dempster were now locked up in the jailhouse. The other gunman, Eustace, and Benjamin were dead; two other men had been badly wounded.

'You should be relieved that we stopped a bad incident from getting even worse.'

'You didn't.' Hague leaned back against the wall and took a sip of his drink. 'Your incompetence let a minor disagreement turn into a bloodbath that's left two men dead.'

'I regret how the incident ended, but we did everything we could.'

Hague shook his head, then slammed his mug down on the stove. He marched across the law office to face Rattigan. He raised a hand and counted off his points on his fingers.

'You let known troublemakers back into the saloon. You failed to check that they weren't armed. You let an argument with Benjamin Graham develop. You let your prisoners escape and shoot up the saloon. Worst of all, you didn't call for me.'

Hague set his hands on his hips, defying Rattigan to rebut his allegations.

'I take full responsibility for what happened,' Rattigan said, settling for a politic response.

'You already have done,' Hague sneered. 'Then again, you always do.'

'At least we can agree on ... '

Rattigan trailed off and narrowed his eyes. 'What's that supposed to mean?'

'Only what I said, that you always take responsibility for your mistakes; but that's no comfort to the men who end up dead, is it, Marshal? Or, to give you your full title, the marshal of Idiot Creek.'

Rattigan gulped. 'Ex-marshal, as I'm sure you now know.'

'And that's about the only good thing I can see about this situation. At least you're no longer dishonouring the badge.'

Hague tapped the star on his chest and then walked back to the stove where, with his back turned to Rattigan, he sipped his coffee.

'Who told you?'

'I heard some gossip, and this time it was true.'

'Then, for the record, you probably heard a version of the story of my downfall rather than the truth.' Rattigan waited for a response, but Hague said nothing. 'But I guess you don't want to hear that. So, if you have no more questions, we have a job to do.'

'No, you don't.' Hague turned round. 'The Sagebrush saloon no longer needs your services.'

'That's not your decision to make. The owner, Martin Fox, employed us. Only he can tell us to leave.'

'You're right, but bearing in mind all the trouble there this afternoon and the fact that I told him what I'd heard about you, I reckon you shouldn't waste your time heading back to the saloon.' Hague smiled. 'As before long everyone in town will know about you, you shouldn't stay in Redemption either.'

'You told Martin about the lies you'd heard about me!' Rattigan snorted. 'You may have contempt for my record as a lawman, but I sure never stooped to your level.'

Hague only shrugged. As it looked as if he'd get the last word, Rattigan headed to the door. Callan followed close behind, although Schneider didn't join them.

Schneider spoke to Hague. Rattigan couldn't hear what he said, but he assumed he was making a case for his being treated differently.

Rattigan couldn't blame him. After all, unlike himself and his former deputy, Callan, Schneider wasn't a disgraced ex-lawman; as they'd recruited him only a month ago, Rattigan assumed that he had been unaware of their shared past.

The two men stood on the boardwalk, looking down the main drag towards the saloon, but Rattigan didn't welcome the thought of confirming that they were no longer welcome there. He turned to Callan, who shrugged.

'I guess we were lucky to last this long before someone worked out who we were,' Callan said.

'We were.' Rattigan sighed. 'Six months ago we decided to head west until we found somewhere where nobody knew about us. It seems we haven't travelled far enough yet, so we need to move on and try again elsewhere.'

'I agree, but Redemption is the third

town we've tried and I was starting to think we could settle here.' Callan looked to the west. 'Worse, we're on the edge of the Barren Plains and that means there's nowhere to move on to.'

Since the railroad had now arrived in Redemption they had plenty of options for an easy passage out of town, but Rattigan didn't disagree with Callan's downbeat assessment of their prospects. Instead, he stood quietly until Schneider emerged from the law office, his scowl suggesting that he'd had no luck talking the lawman round.

'I spent a month working for you,' Schneider said. 'All that time I didn't know that you're worse than the men I threw out of the saloon.'

'When you let Vick into the saloon you told me that every man deserves a second chance,' Rattigan said. 'So perhaps you should prove you mean that by judging me on the past month and not on whatever rumours you've heard.'

Schneider shook his head. 'I judge a man by his actions; all that matters to me is that because of you I no longer have a job.'

'You no longer have a job because of your failings. In there I took responsibility for the actions of everyone who worked for me and Callan sure didn't do anything wrong. I can't say the same for you.'

Schneider raised a finger to point at him, an angry retort clearly on his lips, but then with a wave of the hand he dismissed the matter and turned on his heel. Together, Callan and Rattigan watched him walk away.

'He didn't reply because he didn't have an answer,' Callan said. 'You were right that he made a whole heap of mistakes back in the saloon.'

'He did, but then again the marshal was right, too. No matter who was to blame, that won't make no odds to Benjamin Graham.'

On that sombre note they made for the station. When they found out that the next train wasn't due until noon tomorrow they sought out a quiet saloon on the edge of town.

Although enough time had passed for news of the events in the Sagebrush saloon to have spread around town, none of the customers looked at them oddly or questioned them about the incident, and so they sat at a table by the window.

For the next few hours, in a desultory way, they discussed their options. They came up with nothing other than to do what they'd done three times already: find another town, look for suitable work and hope that nobody had heard about their past.

They were considering heading to the hotel where they were lodging when the one person they didn't want to see again before they left town came into the saloon; it was Schneider and he had company.

Schneider looked around the saloon room until he saw them. Then he and his companion came over to their table.

'This is Lester Thompson,' he said. 'He was Benjamin Graham's business partner, so I went to him to offer my apologies.'

Rattigan leaned back to contemplate Schneider, giving him a chance to acknowledge that they hadn't parted company on the best of terms, but Schneider didn't meet his eye, so Rattigan kicked out a chair. Lester sat down and, while Schneider fetched another chair, he shuffled up to the table.

'And I accepted them,' Lester said. 'There was nothing you men could have done to save my partner Benjamin.'

Rattigan and Callan murmured their approval of this attitude, while Schneider smiled.

'Once we'd discussed that, we moved on to other matters,' Schneider said. 'And it seems that Lester is looking for three men to do some work for him.'

Rattigan kept his expression stern, the time that he'd spent discussing their next actions with Callan having put him in the mood to treat with scepticism an offer of work in Redemption.

'We lost our jobs after the shoot-out

in the Sagebrush saloon. When the marshal learned that we had a troubled past, he made it clear we're no longer welcome here.'

Lester smiled. 'As I said, you're the right sort of men to help me out. I have a job that nobody wants to do.'

Rattigan narrowed his eyes. 'Yesterday Vick and his colleagues got into an argument with you and Benjamin about work. Did it, by any chance, involve this job that nobody wants to do?'

'It did.' Lester frowned and looked away, suggesting he didn't want to discuss the details. 'Others offered their services, but we didn't reckon they were the sort of men we needed.'

'In that case, the work sounds ideal.' Rattigan laughed. 'What is the job?'

'We're responsible . . . I'm responsible for ensuring supplies are delivered to the Bleak Point silver mine, and another consignment needs to leave tomorrow morning. That means a journey of at least eight days across the Barren Plains and the same time to get back. As you know, there's no water, no shade and nothing for anything to live on out there, and there's nothing to do other than let the sun slowly bake you dry.'

Rattigan nodded. 'That sure is a tough journey to make. What happened to your usual workers?'

'The miners are using up more supplies these days. A wagon used to head there once a month, but Frank Holmes at the mine has asked for a faster turn-around. Now, as soon as the wagon returns here I'll have to load it up so it can set off again. With no time to rest up I've struggled to find anybody who wants to make the trip, and the next delivery is now overdue.'

Rattigan looked at Callan, who gave a slight inclination of the head while glancing at Schneider. Getting his meaning, Rattigan turned to his former colleague.

'I'd guess that on a journey across the Barren Plains it's important to trust everyone in your group.'

Schneider gulped and shuffled on his chair before facing Rattigan.

'I thought about what you said about every man deserving a second chance,' he said. 'You were right. For the last month you've been a good boss and you did try to take responsibility for my mistake.'

'I'm pleased you see it that way now.'

'Now that I think about it, I accept I underestimated Vick and the other men. I let them into the saloon and I didn't keep my prisoner under control.' He shrugged. 'But if you can overlook my mistake today, I can ignore whatever you did wrong six months ago.'

Rattigan glanced again at Callan, who nodded.

'The silver mine sounds like it might be a lucky place for us,' Callan said.

Rattigan smiled and held out his hand to Schneider.

'In that case, it looks as if Callan and me will be heading to Bleak Point,' he said. 'And I've heard enough to accept that we can continue to work together.'

Schneider glanced at the hand. 'I agree, but I reckon you've misunderstood Lester's offer. On this job we won't be working together. You'll be working for me.'

Schneider watched as Rattigan winced and then took his hand.

3

The three men met up outside Lester Thompson's mercantile at sunup.

The long open wagon was already standing on the main drag, so their first task was to load the supplies. Schneider immediately took command.

Speaking in clipped tones, and with much arm waving, he ordered Rattigan and Callan to deal with ferrying the piles of crates and sacks from the store to the wagon. He allocated himself the task of marking off the inventory and ensuring everything was accounted for.

Whenever they took a new load out of the store Schneider barked unnecessary encouragement at them. This early confirmation that he intended to take his new role seriously made Rattigan and Callan exchange amused glances. But by the time they had completed the task both men had grown tired of

Schneider's excessive posturing and his failure to help them with the heavy lifting.

'There's still time to change our minds,' Callan said when he and Rattigan were sitting on the driving seat. 'The train is due at noon and we could still get on it.'

While giving the matter serious consideration, Rattigan watched Schneider consult with Lester.

'We came to Redemption because it was an ideal place to stay,' he said. 'This way gives us the option of keeping our base here while being elsewhere most of the time.'

'And if things don't work out, we can always leave Schneider in the Barren Plains and he can make his own way back to town.'

Rattigan firmed his jaw. 'Have some respect, Callan. You're talking about our new boss.'

Callan looked at Rattigan until Rattigan cracked a smile. Then both men laughed at the grim humour, and when Schneider joined them on the seat they both had no trouble in smiling at him.

'What are your orders now, boss?' Callan asked, hunching his shoulders in a suitably subordinate manner.

Schneider regarded both men with narrowed eyes and then pointed ahead.

'I got all the directions I need from Lester. So now, move us out.'

Callan took the reins and shook them to move the horses on.

'What are those directions?' Rattigan asked.

'There's no need for you to know that. You only have to worry about following my orders.'

'Understood, boss,' Rattigan said with a sideways glance at Callan.

Schneider drew in his breath through his nostrils, but he didn't retort. Then, at a steady pace, they headed through town and on towards Redemption Gorge.

The railroad was being built through the gorge, after which it would carry on across the Barren Plains to Bleak Point, an endeavour that, when completed, would remove the need for the task they were carrying out now.

Bearing in mind all the construction work taking place, Schneider directed them to skirt across the mouth of the gorge and then head to the east so that they could avoid the railroad workers. Then they tracked along lower ground until they could head north again towards the Barren Plains.

Despite the irritating start to their journey, which had suggested that Schneider would use every opportunity to reinforce the fact that he was in charge, the day passed quietly. By the time they settled down for the night they were acting in the same relaxed way as they had adopted while working at the saloon.

When they camped down Schneider still delivered unnecessary orders, but his attitude no longer annoyed Rattigan. He had no trouble in remaining calm when, after they had eaten and they were sitting around a campfire, Schneider asked the question Rattigan had been expecting since yesterday.

'So what happened to you six months ago?' Schneider asked.

'Marshal Hague will have told you the basics,' Rattigan said. 'Everything he'll have said is true.'

'Except I reckon your version of events will be different and, as I have to judge whether I can trust you to complete this job, I'd welcome hearing how you ended up being called the marshal of Idiot Creek.'

Rattigan pursed his lips and then warmed his hands before the fire while he put his thoughts in order. He decided to provide the answer he'd given several times already, which covered the incident with the minimum of details, even though that version had yet to convince anyone that he had been treated unfairly.

'I was the town marshal of Ash Valley and Callan was my deputy. I had an informer, Woodrow Albright, and he told me that a lowlife bandit called Jasper Minx planned to raid a train on the bridge over Idiot Creek. So Callan and me holed up by the bridge, but the train passed by without a hitch.'

Schneider nodded. 'So Woodrow had lied?'

'Woodrow was a good-for-nothing jackal, but he'd always been reliable before. I guess he'd drawn me in and taken me for a fool.' Rattigan leaned forward to pick up an unburnt branch, broke it in two and threw one half on the fire. 'When we followed the train back to Ash Valley the town was in turmoil after Jasper's bank raid.'

Schneider gave a sympathetic frown. 'How much did Jasper steal?'

'Not much. The townsfolk stepped in and fought him and his bandits off, but two men paid the price for their bravery and for my mistake.'

Rattigan threw the second half of the branch on the fire. 'Afterwards, I lost the confidence of the town.'

'So they didn't accept that Woodrow should take the blame?'

Rattigan shook his head. 'Woodrow had high-tailed it away from town with

Jasper and my explanation about his involvement only made things worse, as nobody could believe I'd trusted the word of a man like him.'

Rattigan looked at Callan to see if he wanted to add anything more. After a moment's thought Callan nodded.

'Maybe if Woodrow hadn't sent us to a place called Idiot Creek,' he said, 'everyone's contempt might have been less and we could have ridden the situation out, but before long it became impossible to stay on in Ash Valley.'

'And so Woodrow and Jasper got away with what they did?'

Callan nodded. 'We'd heard that they'd headed west. So when we set off to look for a new life, we went west, too. We sought out work where we could question travellers, but we've never come across any information about them and neither have we been able to outrun our past.'

'Working at the Sagebrush saloon would have been an ideal way to overhear something about Jasper Minx, but this job won't help your quest,' Schneider pointed out.

Callan shrugged. 'If the silver mine is as desperate a place as we've been led to believe, maybe someone there will know something about Jasper and give us a lead.'

Schneider smiled. 'He could even be there.'

'We're due to get a spot of luck some time soon,' Rattigan said, a sorrowful shake of his head showing that he thought this was unlikely. 'But we've accepted that tracking down Jasper will take a long time and we'll have to explore plenty of unpromising places before we find out where he's gone.'

Schneider rocked his head from side to side and then shrugged.

'I can see why people got annoyed with you, but none of that sounds too damning,' he said. 'I reckon that despite your mistake, I should give you a second chance.'

Rattigan tensed, but he forced himself to return a smile.

'And I reckon you should get a third chance, too,' he said.

'Third?' Schneider said.

'You made your first mistake yesterday in the saloon when you failed to follow my orders. You made your second today when you proved that giving orders isn't as easy at it looks.'

'I've done nothing wrong today.'

'That's your opinion, but this morning you wasted a lot of time and effort ordering us around when you didn't need to. Then you kept the directions we'll follow to yourself, and that's — '

Schneider pointed a stern finger at him. 'Your role on this job is the same as Callan's was when he went with you to Idiot Creek. You do what I tell you to do, even if what I tell you to do isn't right.'

Rattigan nodded slowly while Callan muttered something under his breath, but both men resisted the urge to continue the argument.

'So what are our orders for tonight?' Rattigan said after a while.

'The next few days will be the most dangerous. Raiders often lurk around the edge of the Barren Plains, waiting for people like us to come along. Once we're further into the plains they won't trouble us, but right now we need to be careful. You'll take the first guard duty.'

'And who'll take the second duty?'

Schneider smiled. 'There are only two of you. So I'll let you figure that one out for yourself.'

Schneider then settled back against his saddle, his hands behind his head in an obvious gesture of making himself comfortable before he rested up for the night.

Rattigan glared at Schneider, but when Schneider didn't look at him again, he stood up and searched for a suitable location in which to stand guard. Callan joined him and they moved away to a patch of elevated ground fifty yards from the camp.

'Have you changed your mind about my earlier suggestion yet?' Callan said when they'd agreed it was a good spot.

'We can always find somewhere to leave Schneider and let him walk back to town.'

'If he doesn't change his attitude we won't be leaving him afoot,' said Rattigan.

Callan furrowed his brow.

Rattigan gestured ahead at the route they would take tomorrow where the land became increasingly stark.

'The Barren Plains is a huge place,' he went on. 'I doubt anyone would ever find his body.'

Callan laughed. Then, as they had heard the same tales about raiders preying on the railroad travellers and anyone else heading this way, they set about agreeing their schedule for the night.

As it turned out the night passed peacefully. As they had often carried out duties like this when Callan had been Rattigan's deputy, by allowing them both the opportunity to relax the night had the opposite effect to what Schneider presumably hoped to achieve.

So, when they set off the next morning and headed deeper into the plains, Rattigan was in good spirits. That happier frame of mind didn't last for long.

As the day wore on the heat built up. With no shade to provide relief in the bleak terrain none of the group was left in any doubt as to why the area had been called the Barren Plains.

They stopped frequently to rest the horses, but the lack of anything else to do gave Rattigan plenty of opportunities to doze. The heat ensured it wasn't a restful sleep.

By sundown they had passed beyond the far end of Redemption Gorge leaving only flat ground ahead of them. Occasionally Schneider referred to the map and the notes he'd received from Lester. As there were no obvious landmarks, Rattigan assumed he was navigating using the sun, but he couldn't confirm this as Schneider kept the map to himself.

The long day had removed Rattigan's

desire to argue with Schneider. When they settled down for the night he accepted his orders for the evening without complaint.

With no change in their circumstances and little to occupy their minds, everyone then settled into a routine, and for the next few days they travelled without incident.

When they reached the halfway point in their journey Redemption Gorge had disappeared from view behind them and they could now see the distant spire of rock that identified their destination of Bleak Point.

This first sighting of the location of the silver mine made Schneider sigh with relief, suggesting that he hadn't been as confident about his ability to navigate as he had been trying to suggest. Consequently he was more animated that night, so Rattigan chose this moment to speak up about their night-time duties.

'We're some distance from Redemption,' he said. 'At least from now on we won't have to worry about raiders.'

'I'm sure you're right that we don't have to worry about opportunist raiders, but there's still the other concern,' Schneider said.

Rattigan waited, but Schneider didn't amplify.

'Which is?' Rattigan prompted.

'When I took responsibility for this duty, I spoke with Marshal Hague. He reckoned that as Eustace had done all the shooting in the saloon, he'd have no option other than to release Vick and Dempster, although he did plan to make sure they left town.'

Rattigan nodded. 'And as they have a problem with us and with the mercantile, it's likely that they could then come looking for us.'

'They'd be foolish to follow us all the way out here, but then again they didn't strike me as men who had much sense.'

Rattigan couldn't argue with that, so he didn't object to Schneider's order to continue keeping watch. Again the night passed peacefully, but in the morning Schneider was still agitated.

He kept looking around as if, by having spoken about his concern last night, he had succeeded only in worrying himself even more.

'The thing about this flat terrain is that we'll see any trouble from far away,' Rattigan told him as they prepared to move the wagon on.

When Schneider still looked concerned Callan moved forward.

'He's right,' he said. 'The biggest danger comes in the night, and we saw nothing to concern us last night.'

'That's what the marshal of Idiot Creek and his deputy think, is it?' Schneider said. 'Well, I reckon I understand men like Vick and Dempster better than you do. If they attack they'll do it when we're at our most vulnerable.'

'And you reckon that's now?' Rattigan asked.

'That's right.' Schneider gestured ahead. 'I reckon they'd find somewhere to hole up a short way ahead and then burst out and surprise us.'

Callan peered along the route ahead,

shook his head and looked at Rattigan, who shrugged.

'You're the boss,' Rattigan said. 'If that's what you reckon could happen, just tell us what you want us to do to counter an attack.'

Schneider rubbed his jaw, looking around in all directions before pointing towards Bleak Point.

'We'll start a new procedure for moving out in the morning. I'll take the wagon on for a couple of hundred yards while you follow on foot, keeping low. If they're out there and that's their plan, we'll soon know if I'm right.'

'And we'll soon know if you're wrong.'

Schneider smiled. 'In this case, I'll settle for being wrong.'

Rattigan returned the smile. 'It's taken a while, but that's the first thing you've said on this journey that does make sense. Head on at a slow pace to draw them out and we'll keep lookout.'

Schneider nodded and jumped on the wagon. As he moved the wagon on,

Rattigan and Callan stood together. Then, without discussion, they drew their guns and split up so as to cover the area from where an attack might come.

Rattigan still didn't believe that if Vick and Dempster had followed them they'd try this tactic, but he accepted that caution was needed. So he peered at every rock and mound of sand ahead in his search for likely places where the men could have gone to ground.

He saw nothing untoward and after pacing along behind the wagon for five minutes he was even more sure that a raid wouldn't be launched. He swung back in towards the wheel ruts and joined Callan, who with a shake of the head silently reported a lack of anything to concern them.

Schneider was travelling slowly, but as Rattigan and Callan were walking he had pulled a hundred yards ahead of them. So far he hadn't looked back and, sighing, both men continued to plod on after the wagon.

'How far do you reckon he'll make us walk?' Callan asked.

'Hopefully only until Vick attacks the wagon, or we'll be walking all the way to Bleak Point,' Rattigan said. Callan laughed.

They trudged on, but after walking for another five minutes Schneider was showing no sign of ending their cautious start to the day; if anything he'd moved even further ahead of them.

Rattigan was thinking about calling to him when Schneider turned in the seat. He looked around, then faced them.

He raised a hand, then turned to face forward again.

'Was that him calling an end to this?' Callan said.

'I don't know, but I sure am. This has — ' Rattigan broke off as with a crack of the reins Schneider hurried the wagon on.

'He's going to make us run to catch up with the wagon,' Callan said. He slapped his hat against his thigh in a show of irritation.

'Could be,' Rattigan said as the wagon continued to speed away, 'but right now it looks to me like he's planning to abandon us.'

4

'Come back!' Callan shouted even though it was clear now what Schneider was doing.

Because of the sandy ground and the heavy load the wagon couldn't move quickly, but it could travel faster than Rattigan and Callan could run. They bounded along after it while shouting and waving their arms, but all the time the wagon moved further away.

Rattigan put on a burst of speed and ran ahead of Callan, but he still couldn't match the speed of the wagon. At last, with his breath coming in ragged bursts, he slowed to a halt. When Callan caught up with him, both men stared ahead with their hands on their knees.

Their only hope was that Schneider was teaching them a lesson for being unenthusiastic about following his commands, but with every turn of the wheels that possibility felt more remote.

The final confirmation of what he was doing came when Schneider looked back over his shoulder at them for a moment or two. Then he carried on at the same quick pace.

With a snarl of anger Callan raised his gun and sighted the distant wagon. He loosed off a shot, but the only effect was to make Schneider hunch down in his seat.

Rattigan didn't want to work off his anger and he didn't join in. Callan fired twice more before relenting.

'All this time we've been joking about leaving him,' Rattigan said when he'd got his breath. 'But he's the one who's left us out here.'

'I can't see why he's done it,' Callan said, glaring at the receding wagon. 'We weren't pleased with taking his orders, but we followed them and we sure weren't any surlier than he was when he worked for you.'

'Perhaps he's just paying us back because he blames us for losing him his job at the saloon.' Rattigan sighed and tipped back his hat. 'But whatever the reason, unless he relents and comes back for us, we're in deep trouble.'

'If he comes back now I'll make him pay for this.' Callan gestured with his gun before holstering it. He glanced at the low sun, which was already burning hot. 'And if he doesn't I'll make him pay double.'

Rattigan couldn't argue with that sentiment, but he took deep breaths to quell his anger and help him concentrate on the more pressing problem of what to do now. He looked back over the route they'd taken towards the no-longer visible Redemption Gorge, and then ahead to the just-visible spire of Bleak Point.

'A long journey back to town, or a long journey to the mine?' he said.

'I reckon we should head back. The railroad has moved on for some distance, so we'll meet up with the workers before we reach Redemption.'

They turned to each other; neither man needed to mention that without water they would be lucky to get even halfway to the railroad.

'The way I see it, we know how far we've come and we know we'll be dead before we get there, but we're not sure how far exactly it is to the mine. It could be nearer than we think.'

Callan peered ahead at Bleak Point. 'It could be further, but going that way has an advantage. If we have some luck and Schneider breaks a wheel, we might catch up with him.'

Rattigan liked this way of thinking and without further discussion they set off. Both men watched the diminishing outline of the wagon in the small hope that Schneider was, in fact, not abandoning them but just keeping them walking at a good pace.

Before long, the wagon became no more than a blot in the distance until at last it merged in with the almost featureless terrain. Then, all they could do was follow the wheel tracks towards their distant destination.

As the sun rose higher the heat built

up, forcing both men to slow down. It had yet to reach even halfway to its zenith when Callan stumbled and dropped to his knees.

'This seems like a good time for a short break,' Rattigan said with a smile, and he slumped down beside him.

'Perhaps we should make it a longer one,' Callan said, giving a worried glance at the sun. 'This heat will only get worse and it could kill us before we've gone much further.'

'You're right that it would be more sensible to rest during the day and walk through the night, but there's no shade out here for us to rest under. I reckon we should cover as much distance as we can while we still have the strength to keep moving quickly.'

'All right,' Callan said without much enthusiasm. He got to his feet. 'You're the boss.'

'I am, but your suggestions are still as welcome as they ever were. If we come across some decent shade, we'll hole up until sundown.'

Rattigan stood up and the two men trudged on together.

'And no matter what,' Rattigan said after a bit, 'we're going to live through this and make our old boss pay for what he's done.'

With this thought renewing both men's enthusiasm they walked at a brisk pace. They managed to maintain the pace only for another hour. Then they slowed to a painful dawdle and this time it was Rattigan who dropped to his knees first.

Callan stayed standing. He pointed ahead and to their right.

'It looks like the wind has created a ridge of sand over there,' he said. 'It might offer some shade.'

Rattigan's only response was to hold out a hand for Callan to help him to his feet. Then they moved on towards the ridge.

They walked for another fifteen minutes, but the ridge didn't appear to be getting any closer. Rattigan consoled himself with the thought that this meant it was probably higher than he'd first thought.

Sure enough, during the next few minutes the ridge stood out ever higher against the skyline as they approached it. Some minutes later still they arrived at the bottom of a slope that rose to a height of about twenty feet above them.

They scrambled up to the top. When they got there they saw that the other side of the slope was mostly in shadow. They flopped down on their backs in the relatively cool shade.

After a few moments of relief from the sun they sought out a more sheltered area, finding a spot where the sun had not yet penetrated today, leaving it cool enough to be a bearable place to sit.

Even better, from their elevated position they could see the route ahead. Rattigan hoped he wasn't fooling himself when he reckoned that he could see more of the spire of rock at Bleak Point than he'd been able to see when they were abandoned.

They debated what they should do next. The chance of staying out of the sun while it was at its highest was tempting enough to encourage them to stay where they were. They settled down and, with nothing to occupy their attention other than their plight, both men dozed.

Harsh rays of light forced Rattigan to wake up and he found that the sun had moved around the ridge and had now eliminated the shade on this side.

As the sun was also getting low he roused Callan. They decided to move on, and found that the rest had restored some of their energy, helping them to walk at a good pace.

They tracked to the left and soon met up with the wagon tracks. They followed the ruts, but before long it became clear that the wagon was no longer heading on a direct course towards Bleak Point.

'What do you reckon Schneider's doing?' Rattigan asked as he put a hand to his brow, shading his eyes so that he could follow the route that the wagon appeared to have taken.

'He had a map, so perhaps he's veering away from the ground ahead for some reason,' Callan said. He shrugged. 'Or perhaps he's worried about us catching up with him and so he's trying to throw us off his trail.'

Rattigan, cheered by this positive thinking, slapped Callan on the back. When they moved on they walked away from the tracks and headed straight for the spire of rock. They took only one more rest before the sun set, then, with a chill setting in, they walked purposefully onwards.

As the darkness grew they picked out stars and, while the spire was still visible, worked out where it stood in relation to the North Star. So, when full but starlit darkness enveloped the plains, they were confident that they were heading in the right direction.

After the fierce heat of the day the cold was welcome. Rattigan managed to keep his thoughts from dwelling on his aching legs and his thirst. Late into the night the moon rose and, hopeful with the extra light, he peered ahead trying to discern Bleak Point.

He couldn't see their destination, but his hopes grew that, with the progress they were making, when daylight returned he would be able to see a significant change in the position of the spire of rock.

First light destroyed that hope.

Despite walking non-stop through the night, Bleak Point looked only slightly closer than it did when the sun had set; he reckoned they would still have to walk for several days before they reached it. The possibility of their being able to do that was remote and it felt even more remote when the sun rose and the heat built up again.

Now, as he and Callan stumbled along, all Rattigan could think about was his parched throat. Within the hour it was so clear that they were making but slow progress that Rattigan didn't object when Callan, espying another ridge of sand, suggested they should again call a halt.

This ridge wasn't as high as the one they had rested behind the day before but it provided enough shade for them to find a relatively cool spot. Rattigan closed his eyes and immediately fell into a restless sleep.

Troubling dreams filled with flames and the unforgiving terrain overcame him, but he only woke up when Callan nudged him in the ribs.

'Just a while longer,' Rattigan croaked.

'No,' Callan said, his voice grating. 'I've been trying to wake you for a while.'

Rattigan sat up and swayed as the sudden movement made him feel light-headed. The sun was already dipping below the horizon, so he'd been unaware of his surroundings throughout the whole day.

The sleep hadn't rested him. When Callan dragged him to his feet Rattigan stood stooped over, feeling his head throbbing, and he had to force himself to take his first step.

Even then he stumbled; Callan had

to hold him up before he was ready to try again. This time he took a full step and at last they set off for the spire of rock, which still looked as out of reach as it had done when he went to sleep.

Without the hope that had lightened their step the previous night, they trudged along, and when full darkness arrived once more it seemed that every undulation in the ground made them stumble.

Rattigan reckoned they were covering ground at only a fraction of the speed that they'd achieved before and even then they only managed by taking frequent rest breaks.

At first their rest periods were brief, but by the time that the beam of light was growing along the eastern horizon they were resting up for longer than they managed to walk.

As Rattigan had feared, when the pre-dawn light grew stronger Bleak Point looked as far away as it had ever done. Worse, when the sun rose and the heat built up again, he couldn't fight off the gut-wrenching thought that they would never reach it.

They staggered on, accepting that if they rested up throughout the day they might no longer have the strength to move come sundown.

Before long Rattigan had to struggle to make his eyes focus on their distant destination. He tried to check with Callan that they were heading in the right direction.

He couldn't force the words out of his baked-dry throat and was forced to use gestures. When he didn't get a response he turned, only to find that Callan was no longer beside him.

He thought back, but he couldn't remember when he'd last noticed him. He cast his gaze in every direction but only flat, featureless ground surrounded him.

With a groan of despair that rattled his chest he dropped to his knees and keeled forward on to his front. He lay peering at the sand beside his face, then tried to raise himself.

His arms refused to obey him; after raising his shoulders for no more than a few inches he flopped back down again. He closed his eyes and listened to his breath wheezing in and out of his larynx, figuring that as long as he could hear that he must still be alive.

For a long, immeasurable period of time he lay there.

He had no idea how long his torment would continue before death took him, so he flexed his fingers and inched them towards his holster. He had yet to touch leather when something made him stay his hand.

Disgusted with his fatalistic thinking he opened his eyes and looked for a scrap of shade. To his surprise a wide pool of shadow was only a few feet away.

He thought through the movements he'd have to make to drag himself into its coolness but then, to his bemusement, the pool of shadow moved towards him until it blanked out the sun. Relieved, he summoned the strength to roll over on to his back.

Rattigan peered up and found that a man was looming over him. The man stood with a sun halo around his wide-brimmed hat and his arms held wide apart to spread out his long coat.

'Didn't anyone tell you that the Barren Plains isn't a good place to take a stroll?' he said.

5

'Who are you?' Rattigan croaked when the first slug of water had lubricated his parched throat.

The man had dragged Rattigan into a depression in the ground. There he had left him for a while before returning with Callan.

Both men were now resting up in the shade on one side of the depression while their saviour sat on his haunches watching them.

'I think of myself as being the walker of the Barren Plains,' he said.

'I can't call you that. Will you settle for Walker?'

The man smiled. 'I will. Now, don't waste your energy on questions. Just rest.'

Walker's eager expression suggested that even if he didn't want to answer questions, he had plenty he wanted to ask the pair of them, but Rattigan reckoned his advice was good. He passed the water canteen to Callan, who sipped the water and returned it to Rattigan.

When Rattigan had again taken a mouthful of water he was able to accept that he wasn't dreaming about enjoying a miraculous rescue, and he let his head settle back on the ground.

His eyelids felt heavy and knowing that he'd struggle to stay awake, he closed his eyes. The next he knew was that Walker was raising his head and forcing him to drink again.

He gratefully gulped a mouthful, then lay back down only to find that he was again being raised up.

'Leave me to rest,' he murmured.

'It's been two hours since you last drank,' Walker said.

Rattigan hadn't been aware that time had passed, but he gulped more water. This time he stayed awake for a while before again dozing. When he next woke up he did so of his own volition and was surprised to find it was now dark.

Walker must have noticed him stirring as he came over with more water before again letting him sleep. The next time Rattigan opened his eyes it was to daylight.

Walker was now standing halfway up the side of the depression, from where he could look out. Rattigan got up to join him; his pain-racked and stiff movements made Callan stir.

'You saved our lives,' Rattigan said as he stretched the tightness from his limbs. 'We're both obliged that you came across us when you did.'

'I'm pleased I could help.' Walker looked him over. 'You look like you're in a better state than you were in when I found you. Are you ready to move on?'

Rattigan looked at Callan, who was now standing up and flexing his back. When Callan nodded, he turned back.

'We are, although we'd like to know in which direction that'll be.'

'I'd guess from the course you were steering that you were trying to reach the mine.' Walker waited until Rattigan nodded, then he pointed to the right of Bleak Point. 'I'll get you there, but I have to take a few detours first.'

'What kind of detours are . . . ?' Rattigan trailed off as Walker moved out of the depression.

Without a backward glance Walker set off in the direction he'd indicated. Rattigan waited for Callan to join him, then the two men clambered out of the depression.

'I guess our saviour won't be forthcoming about what he was doing out here afoot,' Callan said as they followed Walker.

'He saved our lives,' Rattigan said. 'If he wants to be secretive, I reckon we should let him be.'

Walker was already twenty paces ahead of them and had adopted a strong pace that was quickly taking him further away. So they speeded up.

At first, in their weakened states,

both men had to struggle to keep up with him and they stumbled frequently, but Walker maintained a relentless pace, so they forced themselves on until they were walking alongside him.

'So why were you trying to reach Bleak Point afoot?' Walker asked after a while.

'We had no choice,' Rattigan said.

Then, as he saw no reason to avoid revealing the details of Schneider's treachery, he told him the story of the events at the Sagebrush saloon and of their ill-fated mission.

He avoided mentioning the events that had led to their working for the saloon, but that didn't appear to interest Walker; he was more interested in hearing about the supplies and whether they thought Schneider would still deliver them.

Neither man was sure, and Walker scowled when they told him that when they'd last seen the wagon tracks they were veering away from the mine. Then they all walked on in pensive silence.

It was noon when Walker called a halt. He had two canteens, one slung over each shoulder, and he rattled one to show it was empty before removing the other one.

'I had to give you a lot of water yesterday and now we're running dangerously low. Drink slowly and make it last.'

He held the half-full canteen out to Rattigan, who took it, gulped down a welcome mouthful and passed it to Callan. When Callan had finished and held the canteen out, Walker shook his head.

'No matter how used you are to being out here, you need to drink as well,' Callan said.

'I do. I'm going to fetch more water now. You stay here and rest.'

With that, Walker turned on his heel and headed away.

For a while they watched him, but there was no obvious landmark for which he might be heading, so they sat down and took the opportunity to empty the sand from their boots.

They settled down in a position where they could look towards the mine and although they had been bearing to the right of it, the outcrop of rock was now distinctly closer. The surrounding elevated land was visible and it looked to be only a few hours' walking away although, based on past experience, Rattigan assumed it would still take them at least another day to reach it.

Rattigan reckoned that even if Walker didn't return they had enough water to last them while they covered most of the way to their destination, so he had no trouble in waiting patiently. As it turned out, an hour passed before Walker came back into sight.

He was carrying three canteens, along with a saddlebag. He kept two canteens and gave them one.

'I thought there was no water to be found out here,' Rattigan said.

'There's water, provided you know where to look,' Walker replied.

Then, without explaining what skills

71

he'd used to fill the canteens, he set off, this time heading to the left of the mine. With a shrug to each other, Rattigan and Callan followed him.

They walked at a steady pace. Several hours later, Walker again called a halt and, as before, he bade them to stay put while he headed away.

An hour later he returned, this time without having collected anything. Without explaining the reason for his detour he indicated that they should all move off. Then they walked until sundown.

Rattigan would have been prepared to continue walking into the night, but Walker directed them into a bowl-like depression in the ground that was similar to the one they'd settled in the previous day.

The ground here had been flattened down, making it look as if someone had camped out here before. Walker sat down and opened up the saddlebag.

He removed several strips of dried beef, which he handed to the pair of them. The strips were so hard and heavily salted that Rattigan had to struggle to chew and then swallow, but as this was the first food to pass his lips in days, he worked on the strips with relish.

'I assume there's food to be found out here, too, provided you know where to look,' he remarked.

Walker smiled. 'I've left caches of food out here. Only I know where to find them, and I'd be obliged if things were to stay that way.'

'We couldn't tell anyone where they are even if we wanted to. We didn't see where you went.'

'I didn't mean that. I don't just want nobody to know about where I collect water and where I left food: I don't want anyone to know that I'm out here.'

'We're grateful for what you've done for us. Even though we have no idea what you're doing and why you want to be secretive, once we reach Bleak Point we'll keep your secret.'

Walker smiled, but he passed up the

obvious opportunity to provide an explanation for his behaviour. Instead, he settled down lying on his back with his hands behind his head.

As they had covered a considerable distance this day, Rattigan was weary; he followed Walker's lead. He chewed thoughtfully on his last strip of beef, but within moments his eyes closed and he fell into a deep sleep.

The next he knew was that sunlight was shining down on him; as he came fully awake he noticed with a smile that he was still clutching the strip of beef. He stretched and stood up, to find that Callan was still asleep but Walker wasn't visible.

He clambered out of the depression and looked around, but he failed to see their guide.

'Gone?' Callan asked when Rattigan looked back down into the hollow.

'Yeah,' Rattigan said. 'It seems that Walker has left just as mysteriously as he arrived.'

'And he was being fairly enigmatic

during the bits in between,' Callan observed.

Rattigan laughed. Then, when Callan had joined him and satisfied himself that they had been left alone, they moved on towards the mine.

They still looked back several times in case Walker had left them only temporarily while he embarked on another secretive expedition, but he didn't appear.

'What do you reckon he was doing out here?' Rattigan asked after a while.

'He knew where he wanted to go and he went directly to each of the places that we stopped at, so perhaps he didn't have a purpose other than to survive out here.'

'Or he hid his purpose because we were with him.'

'Perhaps, but as you said last night, he saved our lives and that's all that matters.'

Rattigan nodded. 'Hopefully, one day we'll get a chance to repay the favour, but only after we've dealt with Schneider.'

Callan grunted that he agreed. Then

they settled into adopting a steady mile-eating pace.

Rattigan's estimate on the day before, that they could reach the mine within a day, proved to be correct. The sun was still above the horizon when they approached Bleak Point.

Around the central pinnacle there was a circle of rock. The sides were several hundred feet high and too steep to climb.

The entrance to the mine was an area where the rock had fallen away. They headed to this gap and without being challenged they walked through the entrance until they came out in a large flat area.

Deep gouges in the rock to their right suggested where the actual mine was. Numerous tents were to their left and more substantial buildings stood beyond the tents.

They couldn't see anyone in the camp, but a man came scurrying out from the buildings and hurried towards them.

'I haven't seen you two before,' the

man called when he was nearer. He identified himself as Grant Barlow. 'Do you work for Benjamin Graham and Lester Thompson?'

'We do,' Rattigan said. The two of them identified themselves. 'Although I should inform you that Benjamin got shot up in Redemption last week.'

'Then it seems you're the bearers of good news and bad news.' Grant peered past them eagerly with his brow furrowed. 'I assume you've left the supplies on the other side of the entrance.'

'We had some problems on the way.' Rattigan's information made Grant gnaw at his bottom lip. 'Does your question mean that Schneider Wilson hasn't arrived yet with the supply wagon?'

Grant frowned. 'We're overdue for a delivery and things are getting tough. If there's been a problem you'd better keep quiet about it until you've spoken to Frank Holmes.'

Grant glanced around. Seeing nobody about he put a finger to his lips to urge them to be cautious and beckoned to them to follow him. He took them across the flat area, past the camp and on to the buildings that included a stable, workshops, and a saloon.

Grant indicated that they should enter the saloon. As it was late afternoon and the miners would still be working, the place was occupied only by one man, sitting at a table in the corner. He was examining a ledger and he held a hand up for Grant to stay back while he completed his task. This gave Grant time to identify him as the mine-owner, Frank.

'You'll be pleased to know that everything is in order,' Frank said while still running a finger down a list of figures. 'Nothing else has gone missing in the last week.'

'At least that's some good news,' Grant said. 'We'll need it. These men, Rattigan and Callan, say that Benjamin Graham was killed last week, and there's been a problem with the next batch of supplies.'

Frank grimaced and looked up at the three men.

'Oh?' he said with a pronounced gulp.

'We had a disagreement on the way here and Schneider Wilson went on ahead with the supply wagon,' Rattigan said, settling for a short version of events. 'We were afoot, so he should have got here by now.'

Frank shook his head. 'We've seen nobody new until you two arrived.'

'I guess Schneider must have encountered a problem and he'll get here soon, but it sounds as if, with food getting short, you're suffering a spate of pilfering.'

'We've been suffering the stealing for a while. That's why I requested a more frequent delivery from Lester and Benjamin. If the next load doesn't arrive soon I reckon our other problems will escalate.'

'What other problems have you been having?'

Frank got up from his table and came across the room to join them. Even then he kept his voice low.

'For the last few months men have been going missing. Miners often suffer terrible ends here, but this is happening at frequent intervals and the bodies have never been found. Five men have disappeared so far. I doubt it has anything to do with the pilfering, but I have no idea who is responsible.'

Rattigan rubbed his jaw; then he smiled.

'It sounds to me like you could use the services of a lawman,' he said.

6

Frank stepped back to appraise Rattigan and Callan.

'I could do with help to solve my problems,' he said. 'I have a team of guards to keep the miners under control and to safeguard the silver, but they don't have the skills to carry out an investigation.'

'We do have those skills,' Rattigan said. 'I was once the town marshal of Ash Valley and Callan was my deputy.'

Frank narrowed his eyes. 'So you're telling me that two lawmen grew tired of keeping the peace and opted instead to look after a supply wagon that's heading across the Barren Plains?'

Rattigan tipped back his hat. 'I don't blame you for being sceptical,' he replied, 'and I can only say that the townsfolk grew tired of us before we grew tired the law. I'll be pleased to tell you the story of what happened, but you'll have to take our word that it's the truth.'

Frank rubbed his jaw and walked about the room as he pondered on these words. Then he nodded.

'I don't need to hear that story. I judge a man by his actions and not by his past. If you can fulfil your promise to get me some answers, I don't care about what you did before you came here.'

Rattigan raised an eyebrow in surprise. 'That's mighty generous of you.'

'It's not. That's the only way a place like Bleak Point can operate. Only the most desperate come to the Barren Plains. Half the miners have something to hide and if I asked questions about their pasts, I'd struggle to get anyone to work here.'

'I can understand that, but if we're going to get you some answers, we'll be asking plenty of questions.'

'You can ask all the questions you want, but you'll only ask about crimes that have been committed here. Anything my workers did before coming to Bleak Point is no concern of the marshal of the Barren Plains and his deputy.'

Frank held out a hand. Rattigan took it without hesitation.

'I reckon we can work under those rules,' he said.

Frank moved on to shake Callan's hand. Then he gestured at Grant, who stepped forward.

'In that case,' Frank said, 'my able assistant will show you around so you'll be prepared when the first batch of miners end their shift for the day.'

Frank nodded to both men and returned to his table. Grant ushered them to the door. They stood outside the saloon while Grant explained the lie of the land. It was as Rattigan had assumed from his brief look around when they'd first arrived.

The miners' camp was to the side of the entrance, while the mine workings were on the other side. The buildings provided living quarters for Frank and his senior staff, as well as premises for administrative tasks, entertainment and dining.

The mention of food made Rattigan's belly grumble and he interrupted Grant's explanations.

'We'll start by dealing with your problem with the supplies,' he said. 'Show me where they're stored.'

Grant nodded and directed them to the end of the row of buildings that was furthest away from the tents. A large store stood against the rock face, while set out beyond the building were long tables; only an overhanging length of rock provided cover from the harsh sun.

Animated activity was getting under way as several cooks bustled about as they prepared for the evening's meal. Two men stood before the door to the store with their arms folded, the suspicious scowls on their faces suggesting that they were guarding the building.

'You'll need to talk to them,' Grant

said, indicating the guards. 'They look after the store at all times.'

As they moved closer to the store Rattigan caught Callan's eye and received a knowing wink from his deputy. This response acknowledged that Callan was enjoying settling back into the routine they had once enjoyed in Ash Valley, and that he'd had the same thought that had occurred to Rattigan.

If supplies had been going missing from a building that was being guarded, either the guards were incompetent or they were involved in the stealing. Rattigan studied the guards with narrowed eyes, wondering which of the two possibilities was the more likely.

He reckoned he had come across the men before, although he wasn't sure when. He sensed Callan tensing up, which suggested he'd had the same thought. Then the nearer of the guards noticed them; he nudged the other man.

The guards looked them over. Then

one man moved to the corner of the building and glanced along the side wall, apparently making an urgent gesture to someone out of Rattigan's line of vision. Then both men straightened up as Grant led the two lawmen towards them.

They were ten paces away when Rattigan figured out why the men were familiar. A moment later he had his assumption confirmed.

Jasper Minx came round the side of the store and stood between the two guards, whom Rattigan now knew to be the Peel brothers: Kirby and Oliver.

Rattigan had never met these three men before, but he recognized them from Wanted posters; now all three of the Jasper Minx gang was here. The three men dangled their hands beside their holsters and the smirk on Jasper's face showed that he knew who he was facing.

'I knew that one day we'd catch up with you,' Rattigan said when the three men spread apart to form a line in front of the store. 'You couldn't run for ever, Jasper.'

'We weren't running,' Jasper said. 'We chose to come here.'

Grant gave a worried grunt as he caught on to the direction this meeting was likely to take, and he backed away. Then he scurried off towards the saloon, calling out for Frank to come quickly.

Rattigan licked his lips and set his feet wide apart.

'From what Frank Holmes said about this place, few men choose to come to the Barren Plains.'

'If you've already spoken with Frank you'll know we're beyond your reach here. The marshal of Idiot Creek can't do nothing to nobody in Bleak Point.'

Rattigan smiled. 'Except I'm not the marshal of Idiot Creek no longer. Fifteen minutes ago Frank appointed me as marshal of the Barren Plains.'

Jasper twitched; Kirby and Oliver glanced at each other, showing concern for the first time.

'We look after security at the mine,' Jasper said.

'And I gather you haven't been doing your job well. Supplies have been stolen and men have gone missing; but that's not the important matter here. You men are wanted for what you did in Ash Valley.'

Jasper smiled. 'Then I suggest you do your duty and arrest us.' He edged his hand towards his holster while the brothers settled their stances.

In response, Callan stood tall while Rattigan rolled his shoulders and bored his gaze into Jasper's eyes.

Jasper was the first to look away; with a sneer he looked past the lawmen. Rattigan didn't move, refusing to let Jasper's defiance distract him, but then footfalls sounded and a few moments later Frank Holmes's voice could be heard.

'What's the problem here?' Frank called.

'I was just discussing your latest decision with Rattigan,' Jasper said, relaxing his tense posture.

Frank moved on until he stood beside Rattigan. He glanced at the two groups of men; his facial expression confirmed that he could see he'd arrived just in time to avert a showdown.

'I assumed you would and there's no need to be concerned. Your duties haven't changed. You're still responsible for keeping the mine safe, and Rattigan will only step in to deal with the aftermath of any trouble you can't control.'

'That sounds reasonable.' Jasper chuckled. 'It means Rattigan won't have to do nothing other than sit in the saloon and watch me and my men take care of things.'

Frank nodded and looked at Rattigan, who took his time in responding. He turn to Frank.

'I have no problem in performing the duties you've laid down,' Rattigan said. 'I have plenty of problems with the men I'll have to work with.'

'I've already gathered you and Jasper have a history, but I hope I don't have to explain again my rule: that a man's past before he came here is no concern of yours.'

'I accept that, but even your generous rule has to have a limit, and Jasper will have exceeded it a dozen times over.'

Frank frowned. 'The other half of my rule is that I judge a man only by his actions here. Jasper has performed adequately and you have yet to prove yourself. If you can't find a way to work with Jasper, you can leave Bleak Point now.'

While Jasper smirked and his men chuckled, waiting eagerly for his reaction, Rattigan chose his next words carefully. Before he could again try to talk Frank round to his way of thinking, Callan stepped forward.

'We accept your ruling and we'll give you no trouble over this,' he said. 'Now, if you don't mind, we'd like to get back to work so we can prove to you that you made the right decision in employing us.'

Frank nodded but kept his gaze on

Rattigan. Rattigan couldn't bring himself to back up his deputy's tactic of mollifying Frank. He glared hard at Jasper, then with a grunt he turned away.

Jasper snorted a laugh and his men followed suit; Frank muttered an admonishment, but Rattigan didn't wait to see what effect the words might have. He moved on towards the tables and then walked alongside them, trying to fight down his anger about the situation.

By the time he reached the final table, he felt no calmer. He sat down on the end of a bench. This position commanded a good view of the area, letting him see that Frank and Grant were now returning to the saloon while Jasper and his men were standing in a huddle beside the store.

The cooks who had been making preparations for tonight's meal were now heading into the store. This reminded Rattigan of how hungry he was.

'We'll stay here until dinner,' he said. 'Then we'll eat with the miners and see what we can learn about the men who have gone missing.'

Callan nodded and sat beside him. 'I'm pleased you're starting to put your mind to the task at hand.'

Rattigan rapped his knuckles against the table a few times, then he turned to his deputy with a sigh.

'You surprised me when you spoke up, but you did the right thing with Frank. If you hadn't spoken sense I surely wasn't going to do it.'

'I could see that, but I'm just as annoyed with this situation as you are.'

'Except you kept a cool head, and I'm grateful for that.'

'I did have some help.' Callan gestured at the store. 'While you were busy getting annoyed with Frank, I was watching the cooks, and one of them is another man we know all too well: Woodrow Albright.'

Rattigan winced and peered at the cooks as they emerged from the store, but he didn't see Woodrow amongst them.

'Are you sure?'

'Yeah, but he saw us and he decided that it was a good time to be elsewhere.'

'So the man who lied and told us to go to Idiot Creek so that Jasper Minx could raid Ash Valley's bank is here as well as Jasper and the rest of his gang.'

Callan nodded. 'We've finally had that spot of luck we've been waiting for. All the people who wronged us six months ago are in one place.'

Rattigan rubbed his jaw. 'That sure makes things interesting, but why did seeing Woodrow help you keep calm?'

'Because that made me accept Frank's rule that everything that happened before we came to the Barren Plains now counts for nothing. However annoying that is, it won't matter none because we are allowed to deal with any crimes committed here.'

Rattigan smiled, now getting Callan's meaning.

'And now that we know that Woodrow, Jasper and the rest are here, we know who's responsible for the stealing and for the unexplained disappearances.'

'Sure,' Callan said, returning the smile. 'We know who's guilty. Now we just have to prove it.'

7

While the work to make the evening meal got under way, Woodrow Albright sloped back to the store. He had tasks allocated to him, but he kept his head down and avoided looking at the last table, where Rattigan and Callan had taken up residence.

Rattigan watched both Jasper and Woodrow, but they didn't converse. Presently miners trailed into sight; this encouraged Jasper to make off for the tents, leaving Kirby and Oliver guarding the store.

It soon became apparent that Woodrow was responsible for cleaning tables and clearing plates, so he would have to struggle to avoid coming close to them for the whole evening. With that observation made, Rattigan and Callan joined the queue for food, after which they returned to their place at the end of the table.

The miners were filling the tables from the other end, so it was some time before they had close company and even then the men barely acknowledged them before they concentrated on eating. Rattigan and Callan didn't mind as they were busy wolfing down their meals and neither man was ashamed to rejoin the queue for a second helping.

They then took their time over eating and when the men near by slipped away from the table and left their plates, it wasn't long before Woodrow had no choice but to approach them for the first time.

He came over, calling out cheerily to various diners in an obvious attempt to appear animated so that he didn't have to catch the lawmen's eyes. When Woodrow piled up the empty plates, Rattigan swept several plates closer to his own and sat back.

Woodrow considered the plates. Then, with a sigh, he looked at Rattigan's face and winced, as if he'd only just noticed him.

'It sure is a pleasure to meet you again,' he said with a breezy air that might have sounded more convincing if he hadn't then broken off to gulp. 'What are you doing out here?'

'Haven't you heard?' Rattigan said. 'I'm the marshal of the Barren Plains.'

'That sure is a responsible position.' Woodrow looked around so that he seemed to address the nearby miners while he spoke to Rattigan, even though nobody was showing an interest in their conversation. 'From what I've heard about you, I'm sure you'll do a good job.'

Then he moved to sweep up the last plates, but Rattigan slapped a hand on his wrist, halting him.

'We'll talk, later,' he said, keeping his voice low. 'I reckon you can help me again with information on Jasper Minx and anything else that's been going on here recently.'

Woodrow gave a worried nod. Rattigan raised his hand, freeing him to collect the plates. Then Woodrow scurried away.

'Now it's your turn to surprise me,' Callan said. 'I didn't think you'd ever want Woodrow's help again.'

'I said I wanted to talk to him, but that doesn't mean I'll act on anything he tells me.' Rattigan winked. 'In fact, the best policy might be to listen to his lies and then do the opposite to what he suggests.'

Callan chuckled. Then they settled down to eat the remains of their second helpings.

By the time they'd finished no new miners were arriving. Once they had enjoyed their meals some miners stayed at the tables to chat amongst themselves, while some others headed back to the tents.

The rest made for the saloon, so Rattigan and Callan followed a group of them inside. The saloon room turned out to be half-full, with small groups sitting quietly around the tables nursing drinks.

They walked up to the bar, where Frank was chatting to the bartender.

He smiled at them with no sign of the earlier tension.

'There are rooms out at the back of the saloon,' he said, gesturing to a door behind the bar. 'You can bed down in there.'

'Obliged,' Rattigan said.

'Don't be. Jasper and his men stay in the miners' camp and I thought it sensible to keep you apart.'

Rattigan nodded. He ordered whiskeys, which they took to the nearest spare table, and for the next hour they watched the miners.

They didn't get the impression that Frank's problems were worrying anyone and they overheard nothing that would give them a starting point for their investigation. So, since they had learned nothing, Rattigan had no trouble in smiling when Woodrow arrived and walked over to their table.

Rattigan ordered him a drink and then sat back to let Woodrow take the lead.

'I gather you're investigating why

men have been going missing,' Wood-row said.

'It's good to hear that you're still as efficient as you ever were at gathering information,' Rattigan replied.

Woodrow shuffled uncomfortably on his chair before replying:

'I hear plenty while I'm clearing tables and I can report that nobody has any suspicions, but it's obvious to me who's behind it.'

Rattigan raised a warning finger. 'Just give us the facts and we'll do the investigating.'

Woodrow glanced around to make sure that nobody was sitting close enough to hear him.

'In that case, over the last four months five men have gone missing.'

Rattigan snorted. 'When did you arrive here?'

'I got here with Jasper four months ago, a week before the first man disappeared.'

Woodrow had spoken in a neutral tone, but he held Rattigan's gaze for several seconds before sipping his drink.

'Tell me about these missing miners,' Rattigan pressed gently.

'That's the interesting thing. None of them were miners. They worked for Frank. Burl Jenkins was in charge of security before Jasper took over; one man guarded the mined silver, one man paid the wages, one man guarded the store, and the last one worked with me feeding the miners.'

Rattigan frowned. 'So you're saying that most of these disappearances have helped Jasper gather more power?'

'Sure.' Woodrow lowered his head, seemingly accepting that his unsubtle, if indirect, accusation would lead to an obvious retort.

'Why are you trying to incriminate your good friend Jasper?' Rattigan said, deciding not to keep Woodrow waiting for it.

'Jasper is no friend of mine,' Woodrow said with a weary air.

'Really?'

Rattigan leaned forward to look Woodrow in the eye; Callan lent him support by shuffling his chair closer to him.

'I told you the truth six months ago. I overheard Jasper planning a raid on the train at Idiot Creek and I passed that information on to you. I wasn't to know he'd change his mind and try to rob the bank instead.'

Rattigan snorted. 'So why can I trust what you're telling me this time?'

'Because I owe Jasper no favours and because I'm risking my life by talking to you.'

'He's already warned you not to speak to me?'

'We've not spoken since you arrived, but I reckon I had a warning two days ago. My friend, Jefford Clancy, who helped me clear the tables was the last man to go missing.'

'Why was that a warning?'

Woodrow knocked back his whiskey and then glanced to either side.

'We'd been asking around about the

people who have gone missing and I reckon we asked too many questions.'

Woodrow rattled his empty glass on the table and then moved off to the bar to order another drink, leaving Rattigan looking at Callan, one eyebrow raised.

'He looks worried,' Callan said. 'Then again, Woodrow can be a convincing liar.'

Rattigan nodded, but he didn't utter a reply until Woodrow returned with a full glass.

'I agree with you, Callan. Woodrow is the least trustworthy source of information I've ever come across. We shouldn't waste another moment with him until he comes up with some proof.'

Woodrow slapped a hand on the table but Rattigan and Callan ignored him.

'Agreed,' Callan said. 'But I reckon he'll provide all the proof we need when his dead body turns up.'

Rattigan shook his head. 'If that happens, it won't point to Jasper being responsible. The other men who have died recently have never been seen again, so we'll probably have to conclude he was killed by one of the many other people he's annoyed.'

Callan rubbed his jaw as if contemplating this suggestion, giving Woodrow a chance to speak up.

'Quit with the tired routine,' he said. 'I've heard it all before.'

'And yet it's not encouraged you to give us any information we can rely on,' Rattigan said.

'I've already told you that six months ago I heard about the train raid and I . . . ' Woodrow trailed off and lowered his head.

When he looked up, Rattigan relented and gave a sympathetic smile.

'So you're convinced that Jasper is behind this?'

'I am,' Woodrow said, reinforcing his conviction with a hand placed to his heart.

Rattigan looked at Callan, who mustered a thin smile of encouragement.

'And the first man went missing after

Jasper arrived, and he was the first man to ever go missing?' Callan said.

'Bleak Point is a dangerous place. Sometimes miners die, but their bodies are always found.' Woodrow looked aside and then shrugged. 'Except, of course, for that one time.'

'What 'one time'?' Rattigan and Callan said together.

Woodrow shook his head and then took a gulp of his whiskey.

'Forget it. That's not relevant.' Woodrow peered down into his glass with his brow furrowed, presenting a befuddled expression that Rattigan didn't reckon he was feigning.

'What are you not telling us?' Rattigan said.

Woodrow sighed and took another sip of whiskey. Then, after taking a deep breath and with his eyes still lowered, he replied in a low voice, suggesting that he was embarrassed about making his revelation.

'Before Jefford disappeared, we both thought we saw a man lurking out on the plains. We asked around, but we got laughed at. Apparently, the miners have a myth about a man who walks the Barren Plains, even though nobody could survive out there.'

Rattigan was glad Woodrow wasn't looking at them as he and Callan exchanged glances.

'So other people have seen this man?'

Woodrow looked up. 'They have, although nobody will talk about it. The myth is that it's Larry Walker.'

'Larry Walker?' Rattigan repeated. He heard Callan's quick intake of breath.

'Yeah. Have you heard of him?'

Rattigan shrugged. 'I might have heard the name before, but I'm not sure where.'

'Larry was Frank Holmes's business partner. He searched for new seams to explore, but last year he argued with Frank and then threatened to walk out of here. Frank laughed off the threat, but they say that Larry did just that, never to return.'

'And no body was ever found?'

'Larry had to have died, but aside from people sometimes seeing things out there, he's not been seen since.'

'Do you reckon you saw Larry Walker?'

Woodrow tipped back his hat and swirled his glass as he pondered on his reply.

'I was sitting on a rock a quarter-mile from the entrance and I'm sure I saw a man standing beside this other rock about the same distance away, but when I got there, he'd gone.'

'I can see why you got laughed at.'

'So can I, except that, later, Jefford saw him, too. I have no idea who the man was or what he was doing, but I reckon that sighting cost Jefford his life.' Woodrow spread his hands. 'That's all the evidence you'll get out of me until I'm the next one to disappear.'

Rattigan picked up his glass and clinked it against Woodrow's.

'Then you can rest easy in the knowledge that if that happens we'll be sure to ask Jasper some searching questions.'

Woodrow snorted a laugh and then hunched over his whiskey, his furrowed brow suggesting that he was thinking about whether he had anything more to add to his story. He appeared to have decided that he hadn't when suddenly and swiftly he knocked back his drink.

'I start work hours before everyone else gets up,' he said. 'So I'll see you again some other time.'

'You know where we sit at meal-times.'

Woodrow nodded and departed from the saloon, leaving Rattigan and Callan gazing at each other in pensive silence. Presently several of the miners at the bar left too, and that encouraged Frank to leave.

'You know what I hate most about dealing with Woodrow?' Callan said as he watched Frank go out through the door behind the bar. 'Everything he says sounds just plausible enough to be true.'

Rattigan nodded. 'And it never turns out to be so true that what he says the next time is plausible.'

'We can probably trust one thing, though. We now know the name of the man who saved our lives.'

'It seems likely that our saviour was Larry Walker, but I doubt whether knowing that will help us prove what Jasper's doing now.'

Callan didn't reply; instead he looked past Rattigan towards the main door. Rattigan turned to see that Jasper was now standing outside.

Jasper was just beyond the doorway, seemingly having timed his arrival to happen just after Frank's departure. He was talking with two men who were standing in the doorway and glancing their way.

Then Jasper slipped away into the night leaving the two men to pace across the saloon room towards Rattigan's table. They came to a halt in front of him and then identified themselves as Quentin and Unwin.

'So you're a lawman,' Quentin said, his raised voice silencing the chatter elsewhere in the room.

'Earlier today Frank Holmes appointed me as marshal of the Barren Plains,' Rattigan replied in an equally loud voice. 'He's concerned that men have gone missing, and he's determined to put a stop to the recent spate of thefts from our supplies. So if you have something to report, I'd welcome hearing it.'

Quentin set one hand on his hip and gestured at Rattigan with the other, suggesting he wasn't in the mood to be mollified.

'I sure do. You're not welcome here, lawman. You and your deputy can go snooping around somewhere else.'

'We're just sitting here enjoying a quiet drink in the saloon.' Rattigan rose to his feet and so, a moment later, did Callan in support. 'But if you want trouble, we'll be glad to oblige.'

Quentin and Unwin looked around. When several customers murmured darkly the two of them smirked with confidence. Rattigan didn't give them a chance to decide what to do next.

Suddenly he jerked forward, grabbed Quentin's wrist and swung him round to hold him with his arm bent halfway up his back, while Callan dealt with Unwin in the same way.

'Get off me,' Quentin said, trying to kick Rattigan's shin with a heel.

Rattigan's response was to thrust Quentin's arm further up his back until he desisted. Then he looked around the saloon room.

Most of the customers were watching the action with surly glares, but no one showed any sign of intervening. Then a stern voice spoke up from the bar.

'You heard what he said, lawman,' the voice said. 'Leave now or you'll be the next one to disappear, never to be seen again.'

8

Still holding Quentin from behind, Rattigan turned to the bar to find that the man who had uttered the threat had already drawn and aimed his gun at him. A murmured comment from a customer identified him as Oscar.

Flanking Oscar were two other gunmen. One of them had aimed his gun at Callan while the other man was edging his weapon from side to side taking in both of them.

'What do you know about the men who have disappeared?' Rattigan said levelly, meeting Oscar's gaze.

'I'm not answering none of your questions,' Oscar said.

Rattigan smiled broadly. 'I'm not asking about anything you've done before you came to Bleak Point. I'm interested only in crimes committed here. If you have nothing to hide about your activities at the mine, holster your gun.'

Quentin squirmed, seemingly realizing that with Rattigan effectively holding him as a shield, if this confrontation escalated he would be in trouble.

Oscar glanced at his two associates. One man nodded and the other man shrugged but, just as it looked as if they were about to back down, a customer at a nearby table leapt to his feet.

'Don't listen to him,' he shouted. 'No lawman is welcome here.'

Oscar looked at the speaker. Rattigan swung round to face him and saw that the man was throwing his hand to his holster. Rattigan pushed Quentin aside so that he could reach for his own gun, but before he could touch leather the man had already drawn.

A gunshot tore out, but it was the last speaker who jerked aside. A growing red bloom marred his side.

The man righted himself and swung his gun round to aim at the shooter, a red-headed man on the other side of the bar, but a second shot tore low into his chest making him double over before he crumpled to the floor.

Then another gunshot blasted, this time from Rattigan's side of the bar. Rattigan couldn't see the second shooter or his intended target as, with cries of alarm, the customers rose from their chairs, seeking to avoid the crossfire and reach a place of safety.

The customers furthest from the bar jostled each other as they made for the door; those who were at the other end of the room scurried to seek safety behind the bar, leaving the rest to knock over tables and drop down shielded behind them.

Oscar and his two men crouched down, swinging their guns to the left and right as they tried to pick out targets.

Since it now looked as if an opportunity to resolve other, personal feuds had taken the attention away from him, Rattigan sought the nearest cover, ducking down behind the table at which they'd been sitting. As he pushed it over on to its side, Callan shoved Unwin away and knelt down beside Rattigan. Both of them peered over the table.

'That's enough!' Rattigan shouted. 'Everyone holster their guns or I'll — '

He didn't get to finish his order as a shot blasted out from a corner of the room; this time enough people had dropped down for Rattigan to see the shooter clearly. A bald-headed man was aiming at the red-headed man while that man was raising his gun to pick out his opponent.

Two shots rang out with only a moment separating them. One slug hit its target: the bald-headed man dropped to his knees, clutching his holed chest.

Even as he was keeling over to lie face down, Quentin and Unwin stepped in to replace him.

They both took aim at the red-headed man. Neither of them got a chance to fire as Oscar and his men blasted lead at them, their shots cutting across their lower chests and making them spin round before they dropped to the floor.

The red-headed man joined in with

the firing. Oscar cast a sneering glance at him suggesting he wasn't one of his men and he was acting on his own, but Rattigan still dispatched him with a deadly shot to the head. Then he joined Callan in turning his gun on Oscar and his men.

Callan downed the nearest man with two rapid shots to the chest while Rattigan blasted lead into the side of the man standing furthest away.

Oscar had enough time to aim his gun at them and blast off a shot that hammered into the rim of their table, but by then both Rattigan and Callan had him in their sights.

They ripped two shots into Oscar's stomach, causing him to stand up straight before a final shot from Rattigan thudded into his heart and toppled him.

The gunfire reverberated in the small room. Then silence descended.

A dozen heartbeats later Rattigan decided that it looked unlikely that any new feuds were about to erupt, so he rapped his gun against the top of the table three times.

'This ends here,' he said. 'Anyone who is armed throw your gun into the centre of the saloon. Anyone who isn't armed keep down.'

He looked around the saloon, seeing only bodies, tables, and cowering customers. He glanced at Callan, who pointed out several men who were still packing guns, but before he could issue more demands the door behind the bar opened and Frank Holmes returned.

'You heard Rattigan's order,' he called. 'Whatever this fight was about, it's now over. Anyone who isn't happy with that can start making the long journey back to Redemption.'

There was some subdued muttering, followed by several brief conversations and plenty of shuffling. Then one man threw his gun to the floor, an act that instigated a rattle of weaponry being tossed into the centre of the room.

After several moments had passed without any more guns being flung down, Rattigan stood up.

'This gunfight didn't need to happen,' he said, addressing the whole room. 'I'm here only to help Frank resolve his current problems. I don't care none about what anyone has done before they started working here.'

'I'm pleased to hear you say that,' a voice said from the doorway.

Rattigan glanced that way to see that Jasper Minx had returned. He was now surveying the aftermath of the mayhem in the saloon with bright eyes and a wide smile.

'I have no problem with saying that because it's the truth. You stop trouble breaking out, and I step in when you fail.'

Rattigan cast a measured gaze around the bodies, but his implied taunt didn't remove Jasper's smile and when Rattigan finished surveying the scene that faced Frank, the mine-owner was glaring at him. Then Frank pointed behind him.

'Leave,' he said simply.

Rattigan figured that an open argument with Jasper wouldn't help to calm the situation down, so he and Callan walked out of the saloon and then on towards Frank's office.

They waited quietly until, ten minutes later, Frank arrived. His expression was still as stern as it had been in the saloon as he paced back and forth in front of his desk looking them over.

'All the men in the gunfight were looking for trouble,' Rattigan said, deciding to state their case before Frank asked them to explain themselves. 'The only loss to the mine is a reduction in the number of dangerous men around.'

'They may have been dangerous, but they were good workers,' Frank said. 'It'll be hard to replace those eight dead men with miners who can move as much rock as they could.'

'If there was a way to stop the shooting before it got out of hand, I don't know what it was. Clearly, tonight a whole heap of different personal vendettas came to a head at once.'

'Except there's never been an incident like this one at Bleak Point before.

Somehow, everyone managed to resolve their animosities using only the occasional punch-up.' Frank stopped pacing and faced Rattigan. 'What changed tonight to make so much violence erupt?'

Rattigan spread his hands. 'I'll accept that our presence didn't help the situation, but then again, as we've all agreed, we're not here to stop trouble breaking out. That's Jasper's job.'

Frank smiled broadly, as if he'd been waiting for Rattigan to shift the blame on to Jasper.

'Normally, Jasper would be in the saloon making sure the night passed quietly, but as you were there he was in the miners' camp. I gather he was explaining the situation and making sure the miners accepted the change so that it wouldn't cause either of you any problems.'

'I'm sure he wasn't!' Rattigan spluttered. 'He was the one who brought Quentin and Unwin to the saloon and pointed us out.'

'Did anyone see him do this?' asked

Frank, his low voice suggesting that he accepted the seriousness of the accusation.

Rattigan thought back, but Quentin and Unwin had been killed and Jasper had stayed outside the saloon.

'No. He was careful to avoid being seen.'

'He was also careful to avoid blaming what had happened on you.'

'He didn't need to divert blame because he'd already seen that you were annoyed with me.'

'Of course I'm annoyed with you,' Frank snapped. 'Eight men are dead and now everyone is angry that I brought a lawman to the mine.'

Rattigan shrugged. 'Lawmen are often unpopular. I can deal with that.'

'Tonight, I saw how you deal with bad situations. In the past Jasper has always resolved similar problems without letting any recriminations rumble on. As a result, you won't find any men who'll speak ill of him. I can't say the same for you.'

'You've got two men here who can sure speak ill of Jasper.'

Frank sighed and turned his back on them. When he turned to face them again he held his hands wide apart.

'So what would you do, if you were in my place?'

'Nothing. With so many men being dead, for a while nobody will have the stomach to start any more gun battles. And, since everyone now knows about the new situation, Jasper can return to keeping trouble at bay and we can devote our time to finding you some answers.'

Frank rubbed his jaw and then nodded. 'Then I'll accept that. Do nothing.'

'I'm obliged.'

'Don't be.' Frank waved an angry finger at him. 'Rest assured that this is your only warning. One more incident of any kind and you two will be heading back to Redemption.'

'Understood,' Rattigan said with Callan echoing his acceptance of the ultimatum.

Frank lowered his head and everyone

stood in silence for several moments until he looked up at the two friends. He raised his hat, ruffled his hair and uttered a weary sigh.

'I don't suppose you've made any progress with that investigation?' he queried.

'We've heard some rumours and theories, but we have no proof yet. After your warning to tread carefully, we'll make sure we're right about our suspicions before we act.'

'Before you act, you'll bring that proof to me.'

Rattigan nodded. Then, as Frank walked back to bis desk, he and Callan went to the door. When they reached it Rattigan stopped and turned.

'There was one matter that could be relevant that you might be able to help us with,' he said. 'We've heard that the first man who went missing here was close to you.'

'Burl Jenkins went missing first and he looked after security. After his disappearance, Jasper took over.'

Frank narrowed his eyes, clearly warning Rattigan not to make another accusation.

'I wasn't referring to him. I was talking about Larry Walker.'

'What of him?' Frank said, barely moving his jaw.

'I've heard that he tried to walk out of here after you and he argued.'

'Then you heard wrong. We disagreed about many aspects of running the mine, but we always found a solution. It pained me terribly when he left. After he failed to arrive in Redemption I searched for months, but I never found out what had happened to him.'

'I've also heard that some people think he's still alive.'

'Larry spent a lot of time in the Barren Plains looking for other places to dig. Somehow he managed to survive, but even he couldn't walk out of here.'

Frank then turned his back and went behind his desk, where he made a show of rummaging through his paperwork.

Rattigan waited, planning to ask him for more details when he should next look his way, but Callan shot him a wide-eyed glare. Rattigan sighed, accepting he'd pushed his luck. Together they left the office.

They didn't speak again until they found the small rooms that had been allocated to them. Callan peered through the doorway at his room, which contained only a cot and a bowl and then turned to Rattigan.

'Frank didn't like that question about Larry Walker, did he?' he said.

'He didn't,' Rattigan said. 'Which means we now have a place to start our investigation.'

9

Despite Rattigan's optimistic thoughts before he retired for the night, in the morning he felt no nearer to working out how the recent events could be connected to Larry Walker. Neither could he see how he could prove that Jasper Minx was responsible for the disappearances.

When he met up with Callan they headed to the dining tables, where most of the morning meals had already been served.

Miners were drifting away from the tables and setting off for the mine; most of them cast aggrieved looks their way while muttering oaths and taunts. Others gave them a wide berth.

To limit the level of contact with the miners, Rattigan made for the end of the furthest table while Callan collected their meals. When Callan joined him he was scowling and he sat down with a worried sigh.

'Did someone spit in our food?' Rattigan asked.

'No,' Callan said, leaning closer so that he could keep his voice low. 'Apparently Woodrow Albright didn't report for work today and he's nowhere to be found.'

Rattigan winced. 'I guess we made him a promise that if that happened, we'd ask Jasper some searching questions. The trouble is, I can't think of any to ask him yet.'

'I doubt Jasper would answer anything we asked him. He's sure to know now that he has Frank's backing and that we're hanging on here by our fingertips.'

Rattigan grunted that he agreed. Then they ate slowly, each man lost in thought.

'So how do you reckon we can prove what Jasper's doing here?' Rattigan asked when he'd finished eating.

Callan forked in a last mouthful and

smiled, his bright eyes hinting that he'd come up with a good idea.

'I reckon we should consider this situation in a different way.' Callan slapped his chest where a deputy's badge had once rested. 'We should remember that even if we don't wear badges no more and our titles are only subject to Frank's patronage, we're still lawmen at heart.'

'Noble words, but what should we do while we're busy being lawmen?'

'We could start by giving up on our plan to find ways to prove Jasper's guilt. Instead, we should investigate and see where that leads us.'

'To Jasper, presumably.'

'Presumably it will, but I reckon we should keep an open mind and consider what we've learnt so far in a dispassionate way.'

Rattigan nodded and tapped his fingers on the table while he pondered.

'The only thing that we can rely on is that someone is living out on the Barren Plains and he could be Larry Walker.'

'Then we should start there.' Callan

shuffled closer and lowered his voice even though all the miners had now left. 'He's surviving using provisions that he's secreted in various locations, and we know that supplies have been going missing.'

Rattigan smiled. 'That's some mighty fine reasoning. Someone here could be helping him to get hold of those provisions, and it could be that this person's activities have been noticed. Then, to protect Larry's secret, people have been killed.'

'That's what I figure.' Callan shrugged. 'Although the problem with this theory is that it doesn't lead us to Jasper.'

'I reckon the clues will ultimately lead us to him.' Rattigan slapped Callan's shoulder. 'But I agree that we should keep an open mind while we set about tracking down Larry Walker.'

'He left us some distance from the mine and I don't welcome another trek across the Barren Plains.' Callan looked thoughtful and then brightened. 'Then again, if we're to trust Woodrow's story,

Larry has been seen recently, closer to the mine.'

Rattigan thought back and then nodded. They left their table in a more positive frame of mind than when they had sat down.

They headed through the buildings and the miners' camp and then on to the entrance, where they looked out across the plains.

Woodrow had told them he'd seen a man while sitting on a rock a quarter-mile from the entrance. The terrain close to the entrance was flat, and they could espy only one likely candidate.

When they reached that rock, another rock, which could be the one that the mysterious man had stood beside, was another quarter-mile on. They headed there, to find that behind the rock there was a depression in the ground.

The area looked similar to the depressions in which Larry had taken refuge, and each man nodded to the other, acknowledging that one element of Woodrow's story had now gained in credibility.

The ground had been trampled down, suggesting that someone often came to this spot.

'It looks like this could be the place where Larry meets the man who is giving him the stolen supplies,' Rattigan said.

'So Woodrow and Jefford could have witnessed one of those meetings,' Callan added.

'And then they paid for their curiosity.'

Rattigan kicked at the ground and found that once he'd broken through the baked-dry surface, the ground beneath was loose. So he started rootling around.

Callan watched him. Then he realized what Rattigan was after. Larry had claimed that he'd secreted provisions in various places, so Callan started scrabbling too, to see if they could find one of Larry's buried stashes.

They worked systemically, starting at the edge of the hollow and then exploring a strip until they reached the other edge. Then they moved apart and worked separately as they widened the strip of land that they were turning over.

Rattigan reckoned that as he couldn't see any obvious markers that signified a buried object, anything Larry had buried must be easy to reach. So they burrowed down for only a few inches, thereby ensuring they could cover the whole area.

They worked for an hour and the growing heat was making both men grunt with the effort when, with an exclamation of delight, Callan dropped to his knees.

Rattigan hurried over to see that Callan had unearthed a piece of canvas. Callan tugged on the canvas, but it didn't yield so they combined forces to scrape away more sand.

The sand repeatedly filled in to cover the exposed area, but after working for a few minutes they cleared away enough sand to reveal an expanse of canvas. Then a length of wood appeared, the sight of which made both men stop working.

'This is getting interesting,' Callan said.

'It sure is,' Rattigan agreed. 'It is starting to look as if more than just supplies are under here.'

They cleared away the sand from the wood and confirmed that the canvas didn't stretch beyond it. Then they worked their way along the wood until they came to a corner where another length of wood was set at a right angle to the first piece.

With this discovery suggesting the dimensions of the structure they were unearthing, they located the other sides of the rectangle of wood. It was around six feet by four feet and when Rattigan tapped the canvas and heard a solid sound, he presumed that the canvas covered planks of wood.

'If this is Larry's work, he's gone to a lot of trouble,' Callan said, standing back.

Rattigan came to stand up beside Callan so that they could work out what they should do next. He paced around the rectangle and saw that there was a projection on one side.

He knelt and felt the projection; he found that he could slip his fingers beneath it.

'This looks like the way to get underneath,' he said.

Callan nodded and moved over to help him, but when Rattigan gave an experimental tug he raised the rectangle unaided. A gap of a foot opened up and Rattigan lowered his head to peer beneath the rectangle. He gave a low whistle.

Rattigan shuffled back so that Callan could see for himself; Callan looked and gave his own low whistle.

'Another entrance to the mine?' Callan asked.

Rattigan shrugged. Then they moved apart so that they could swing up what was now clearly a trapdoor, to reveal the hole that was lying concealed beneath the sand.

The strong sunlight penetrated far enough to reveal a wall of rock on one side with a ladder attached to it.

They knelt and peered down. Before long, Rattigan's eyes adjusted to the change in light level, letting him see the bottom of the pit, which was about fifteen feet below ground level.

They continued to look, but when no more features revealed themselves, Rattigan straightened up and beckoned for Callan to climb down the ladder.

'We need to check out what's down there,' he said.

Frowning, Callan slipped his feet into the hole; when he had managed to rest a boot on one of the rungs he lowered himself down.

It did not take him long to reach the bottom. He peered around. Then, moving cautiously, he shuffled out of view.

A few moments later he returned to the bottom of the ladder. He looked up at Rattigan, shaking his head.

'Nothing is the answer,' Callan said. 'It's certainly not an entrance to the mine. The space down here is not much bigger than what I could see from up there.'

'Are there any supplies or anything else?'

'Nope.'

'Then someone went to a lot of trouble to cover up nothing.'

Callan nodded. He turned about as he took a longer look at the space he was in. When he'd finished, he still shook his head.

'The hole looks like a natural formation to me,' he said. He pointed at a spot on one of the walls. 'A few gouges have been cut into the rock, as if someone had started working on it but soon gave up. Sand is piled around the sides, but I guess that must be leaking down here.'

Rattigan lowered his head to examine the gouges and the sand. Then he raised himself to examine the ground around the hole.

Sand which moved quickly to fill any hole surrounded him, and he judged the opening to the hole to be roughly at the lowest point in the depression. The perimeter of the depression was high and rounded, suggesting a possible answer to the mystery.

'Perhaps the sand didn't fall down there,' he mused. 'It could have always been there and the rest was emptied out and then dumped around the edges of this depression.'

Callan slapped the wall with delight and looked around again.

'That's right. I've heard about sinkholes where the ground opens up under a man and swallows him up. Perhaps this is what one of those holes looks like if you clear out the sand.'

'If you're talking about quicksand, they need water, and there's not much of that in the Barren Plains.'

'I know, but this is different. I reckon the sand forms a crust over a space.' Callan peered around while rocking his head from side to side showing he was piecing together the situation. 'When an unsuspecting person stands on it, his weight makes him break through.'

Rattigan echoed Callan's delight by shaking a triumphant fist.

'I'd presume that when a man disappears into one of those sinkholes, he's never seen again?'

Callan nodded. 'If the hole was as deep as this one is and it was covered over with sand, he'd never get out, and if nobody saw him fall into the hole, his demise would probably always remain a mystery.'

The two men considered each other with smiles on their faces.

'Except it would seem that Larry knows about this sinkhole, and perhaps about others dotted around the Barren Plains, but why would he go to so much trouble to empty out the sand?'

'I don't know, but when we were with him, he sure was being secretive about his activities.'

'He was.' Rattigan pointed at the ladder. 'And unless you reckon you can learn anything more down there, you should get out and we'll think about where this discovery leads us.'

Callan turned round to make a final consideration of the scene, so Rattigan stood up and moved away from the hole. He had taken only a few steps when someone called out from near by.

They had left the mine some time ago and for the last hour they had been preoccupied, so it was possible that someone had been sent to find them. He moved over to the rock that they had first used to identify the site and cautiously peered past it.

He had been right. Two men were heading towards him and they would reach the depression in a few minutes.

They were trudging along with their heads down and they didn't display any sign that they had seen him, but there was no mistaking their identities.

With a grimace Rattigan hurried back to the hole where Callan was now placing a foot on the bottom rung of the ladder.

'Hurry up,' he said. 'Jasper Minx is coming.'

10

'So Jasper knows about the sinkhole, too,' Callan mused.

'Either that or he followed us, but we can't concern ourselves with that now,' Rattigan said.

Callan nodded and then clambered up the ladder. Rattigan held out a hand to help him out of the hole. Then, leaving the trapdoor open, they scurried back to the rock.

Callan took one side and Rattigan positioned himself on the other. Then they raised their heads, but when Rattigan saw Jasper again, he wasn't where he expected him to be.

Jasper was scurrying with his head down, aiming for a spot to the right of the depression, while Kirby was running towards the left-hand side. There was no sign of Oliver, but clearly he'd holed up somewhere where he could see Rattigan, as a gunshot kicked shards from the rock.

Rattigan and Callan ducked, but not before Rattigan saw Jasper and Kirby drop down on to their chests. Callan edged closer to the side of the rock, but two rapid shots blasted into the edge, forcing him to back away.

'Trapped,' Callan said unhappily.

Rattigan laughed. 'I'd prefer to think that Jasper has made the mistake of acting first. Now he's given us all the excuses we'll ever need to take him on.'

Callan acknowledged Rattigan's optimistic take on the situation with a smile before they looked around the depression. With only a brief glance at each other they agreed to split up, with Rattigan hurrying to the side of the hollow nearest the hole and Callan taking the other side.

Both men dropped down on to all fours and fast-crawled up to the lip of the depression. When Rattigan could see the terrain between them and the mine again, Jasper and Kirby had crawled closer, Jasper now being thirty yards away and Kirby being slightly further than that away from Callan.

He still couldn't see where Oliver had gone to ground, so he lowered his head.

'What are you doing out here, Rattigan?' Jasper called.

'I ask the questions,' Rattigan shouted. 'And I want to know what you find so interesting about this patch of ground.'

'I'm only interested in it because Woodrow told you about it and now you've come out here.'

Rattigan snorted. 'I assume he told you that just before you killed him?'

'Woodrow was too valuable for me to harm him. He always informed me about everything that he told you.'

Rattigan slammed a fist on the ground in irritation before he felt calm enough to reply.

'So you're claiming you had nothing to do with his disappearance, or with his friend's Jefford's demise either?'

'Sure.'

'How can I believe that?'

'Because I have no problem with admitting I threatened Burl Jenkins and the other men who have gone missing. Those men stood between me and what I want to get out of Bleak Point, and once I'd explained how bad their situation was, they left of their own accord. Jefford and Woodrow never gave me no trouble, so I didn't threaten them.'

Rattigan reckoned that that confession sounded honest. He looked up briefly to assure himself that nobody else was close by to hear it.

'I'm surprised you've admitted that to two lawmen.'

'It won't cause me no problems. I'm popular with Frank and the miners. You're not. If you accuse me, nobody will believe you and everyone will stand with me. Either way, you won't get the chance to talk.'

Rattigan turned to Callan and mouthed that he'd now heard enough; then he pointed at his gun as an order to begin hostilities. But it was already too late. A gunshot whined and the sand a foot away from Rattigan's side kicked as he was shot at from behind.

Rattigan rolled away from the blast. As he landed on his back, Oliver dived to the ground beyond the other side of the depression. Rattigan snarled as he realized that Jasper had kept him talking only so that the third man could move in on them.

He aimed at the spot where Oliver had gone to ground, but Jasper used the outbreak of gunfire to launch his assault.

Gunfire thundered, making Callan hug the dirt. When he raised his head another burst of gunfire blasted out, making him drop back down.

Rattigan kept his gun steady, but when long moments passed without Oliver making another move, he realized that Jasper and Kirby would now be coming closer. So he shuffled round on to his haunches and, with his gun still aimed at the last place he'd seen Oliver, he stood up and moved on.

Callan also moved position as he scrambled six feet closer to Rattigan before raising himself. Callan swung his gun to the side, indicating that their opponents had moved closer, and then blasted off two quick shots before ducking down.

Retaliatory gunfire rattled as Callan scrambled back to his original position. Rattigan then moved forward into a position where he could no longer see Callan but could watch for Oliver making a move.

One steady pace at a time he edged forward until he passed the hole. Then he headed back up the sloping side.

As he approached the lip of the depression, he lowered his head to ensure that Oliver wouldn't be able to see him. He looked over his shoulder to confirm that the other two gunmen weren't visible, while Callan was poised ready to start firing when Rattigan gave the order.

Rattigan displayed three fingers, but Callan raised a hand in a warding-off gesture and then pointed.

'Someone's coming to investigate,' he whispered. His voice wasn't loud enough for all the words to reach Rattigan, but his exaggerated mouth movements made his comment clear. 'They're on a wagon.'

Rattigan considered for a moment, but he decided that even if people were heading their way, it didn't alter his intention to end the situation with Jasper now. Not wanting to reveal his position to Oliver, he raised three fingers again.

Callan nodded, and Rattigan turned back. On the count of three he thrust his head up and charged up the final stretch of the slope, while behind him Callan started firing.

When Rattigan was able to see the area outside the depression, he failed to locate Oliver at first, and he wasted valuable moments looking at the unoccupied ground. Then Oliver sprang up into view directly in front of him, having been hiding in a hollow beyond the edge of the depression.

Rattigan started to turn his gun on

him, but he wasn't quick enough. Oliver thrust his shoulders up into Rattigan's chest and shoved, seeking to throw him back down into the depression.

Rattigan dug in a heel and stilled himself. Then he tried to turn the tables on Oliver by throwing him on his back.

Oliver resisted his efforts and, standing on either side of the lip of the depression, the two men tussled.

While gunfire rattled behind him, Rattigan made Oliver bend over to the side. Then he raised himself a step higher with the intention of using his height advantage to knock Oliver over.

In retaliation, Oliver set his feet firmly on the ground and twisted. He failed to dislodge Rattigan, but Rattigan's back foot slipped making him slide back down the slope.

With a cry of triumph Oliver thrust his head up and drove on, forcing Rattigan to take another step back. When Rattigan's feet slid even further down the slope, Rattigan released his hold of his opponent and squirmed, tearing himself away from Oliver's clutches.

Rattigan's freedom was short-lived as Oliver climbed up on to the edge of the depression and launched himself at him. He caught Rattigan around the shoulders.

Then, with Rattigan's footing now being insecure, Oliver carried him backwards until Rattigan's feet slipped and they both went tumbling.

Rattigan hit the ground on his side and rolled twice. The worrying thought hit him that they must be close to the hole and he tried to stay his progress, but he was too late.

From the corner of his eye he saw rapid movement as someone scrambled into the depression to take on Callan. Then the wooden edge of the trapdoor and the black hole beyond loomed closer.

Oliver cried out, seemingly for the first time noticing the danger they were in. Then both men rolled over the wood and dropped.

Rattigan thrust out his right hand

and his clawing grasp closed around the wooden strut. The rest of his body carried on down into the hole, but his grip remained firm.

A crunch sounded below him as Oliver landed on the ground. Then he came to rest with his body dangling.

He thrust up his left hand and gathered a secure hold. With a roll of his shoulders he tried to raise himself to clamber out of the hole, but after his jarring tumble down the slope his arms refused to obey him.

Callan cried out in alarm and several shots followed, all sounding only a few feet beyond his view. With the need to act being urgent, he looked down to see how he could manoeuvre himself on to the ladder, but he saw a more worrying sight.

Oliver was lying on his back. His expression was one of pain, his leg was thrust out to the side at an awkward angle, but he was drawing his gun.

Without a moment's thought Rattigan opened his hands and dropped down. He twisted as he fell and so he landed beside Oliver.

Then he pitched forward and went sprawling over his opponent. He kept sight of Oliver's gun and managed to clamp a hand around Oliver's wrist before thrusting his arm to the side.

Oliver groaned and squirmed ineffectually; it was clear that the fall had injured him. Rattigan raised himself with the intention of slugging Oliver's jaw and incapacitating him still further.

This action proved to be unwise when Oliver flexed his shoulder and put all his strength into swinging the gun back towards Rattigan's body. Rattigan strained to stop him moving the arm, so making the gun swing wildly.

Their manipulations squeezed out a shot. Both men tensed, but then Oliver murmured in pain and his head lolled to one side.

Rattigan glanced down to see that the gunshot had slammed into Oliver's chest. The man exhaled one last sigh and then lay still.

Rattigan jumped to his feet. He'd heard no more bursts of gunfire since the volley that had sounded after he'd fallen into the hole, so he listened before putting a foot to the ladder.

'Callan?' he called. That didn't elicit a response, so he raised his voice. 'Is everything all right out there?'

He carried on up the ladder until his head was just below the opening. Then he climbed up three more steps while keeping his head down leaving him standing crouched over on the ladder ready to spring out.

Then, to his relief, Callan spoke up.

'Rattigan, come out,' he said.

Callan's voice sounded strained, but Rattigan wasted no time. He stood up and leapt out of the hole. He turned to where he'd heard Callan while raising his gun, but then he stayed the movement.

Callan was being held from behind and he had a gun pressed against his neck; two other men had already trained their guns on the hole. In a moment they aimed their weapons at Rattigan.

Rattigan snarled, but he noticed Kirby's body lying sprawled face down, as well as a familiar wagon standing near to the depression. With a double-take he registered what he was seeing.

The two men holding guns on him were Vick and Dempster, the men who had started the gunfight in the saloon in Redemption. After all that had happened recently that event now seemed an age away.

Worse, the man holding Callan was the man who had abandoned them in the Barren Plains, Schneider Wilson.

11

'So you've finally arrived at Bleak Point,' Rattigan said, sneering at Schneider. He glanced at Vick and Dempster. 'I can see now why you veered away from the mine and went on a detour. You doubled back towards Redemption so that you could pick up those two.'

Schneider gestured for Rattigan to drop his gun. Seeing that he had no choice, Rattigan complied.

'I did, but I'm here now,' Schneider said with a smirk. 'And there's no need to thank me for saving your life now that Jasper is hightailing it back to the mine in fear for his life.'

Rattigan narrowed his eyes. 'How do you know Jasper?'

'When you told me the tragic story of your demise during our journey across the Barren Plains, I'd never heard of him.' Schneider gestured at Vick. 'But

153

when I caught up with Vick, he gave me the rest of the story.'

'We used to work at the mine,' Vick said. 'We'd set up some deals skimming off money from the miners, but then Jasper arrived. He warned us that if we wanted to stay healthy we'd have to work for him. When men started disappearing we reckoned that was a good time to move on.'

'And that took you to Redemption, where you shot up Benjamin Graham,' Rattigan said.

'We wanted to set up a lucrative new business venture with Benjamin and Lester.' Vick licked his lips and glanced at Schneider, who chuckled. 'With Schneider's help, we can still do that.'

Rattigan considered everyone's demeanour. He noted the relaxed way they were revealing their plans, along with the positions they'd taken up, which let them keep guns on both himself and Callan at all times.

'You've worked together before,' he said.

'Sure,' Schneider replied with a shrug, as if this was obvious.

'So when you let Vick into the saloon you weren't making a mistake. You were helping an old friend to kill Benjamin, and that's helped you to start a new scheme at the mine.'

Schneider nodded. 'If the food doesn't get through, the miners will starve, but Benjamin and Lester were too decent to try to gain from the situation. We have no qualms about renegotiating terms.'

Rattigan glanced around the men; he figured that if he tried to pick up his gun he and Callan would be dead before he laid a hand on it.

'In that case, I suggest you head to the mine and do that renegotiating.'

'We could, except I reckon that if we rode into Bleak Point and made our demands we'd get a bad reception from Jasper and anyone else who he can persuade to fight on his side.' Schneider raised an eyebrow, and when Rattigan acknowledged he was right with a nod, he smiled. 'Our demands will sound better coming from someone else.'

Rattigan snorted. 'I'm not helping you hold the miners to ransom. You'll have to take on Jasper on your own.'

'When I arrived, you and Jasper were blasting lead at each other. Doing my bidding will give you a chance to end that fight.'

'No deal.'

Schneider jabbed his gun into Callan's neck, making him bend his head to the side.

'You need to reconsider, and the question you need to ask is: which one of us do you hate the most, Jasper or me?'

'You.' Rattigan frowned and then uttered a long sigh. 'Although, as you have several guns on us, I guess I could take your message to Jasper.'

'I'm pleased you're seeing it my way.'

Schneider shoved Callan forward to stand beside Rattigan. He walked around them and came to a stop beside Vick and Dempster. He then gave them instructions on what they should do.

His low voice, coupled with his smirk,

suggested that he didn't expect them to do everything he asked. He was right, but Rattigan figured that wasn't important, as Schneider would only expect them to convey his basic request of wanting more money for the supplies; delivering this message would put them in a dangerous situation.

When he'd finished, Schneider stepped behind them and shoved them on.

As they left the depression Schneider was peering at the hole in apparent bemusement, so they walked on quickly before he decided to call them back to ask them about it.

'Things sure are looking up for us,' Callan said when they were halfway back to the mine entrance.

'How did you come to that conclusion?' Rattigan asked.

'Schneider and Jasper, the two men we hate the most, are both here. If we're lucky, before the day is out, we'll have made them both regret ever crossing us.'

Rattigan nodded. 'I like the way you're

thinking, but I reckon Jasper has had enough time to tell everyone his side of the story and turn the miners against us. So we've got to think of a way to survive the next few minutes.'

'He couldn't turn them against us,' Callan said with a rueful smile. 'We had no allies here in the first place.'

Rattigan laughed, then glanced over his shoulder. Schneider and the others had now returned to the wagon. They had already clambered on board ready to leave quickly if Rattigan failed in his mission.

Then he peered ahead at the entrance. They could see through the high rocks on either side and into the mine, where people were moving into view.

These men pointed them out to others, and that encouraged a rush of men to spread out across the inside of the entrance.

In their midst stood Jasper and Frank. Worse, when they started walking through the entrance Rattigan recognized some of the men from the saloon fight last night, their presence adding to the likelihood of their getting a bad reception.

At the sight of this gathering the two of them stopped about fifty yards from the group, causing the men in the mine entrance to glance at each and murmur darkly. Frank stepped forward.

'You have one chance to explain why you shot up Jasper and his men,' he called.

'We didn't,' Rattigan called back. 'We were following clues that might explain what happened to the missing men. Jasper followed us and started shooting. It didn't do him no good as Schneider Wilson arrived and took him on.'

'Is the man who was delivering the supplies with you?'

'Sure.' Rattigan glanced over his shoulder and Schneider chose that moment to edge the wagon forward so that it could be seen through the entrance. 'Those provisions are now here.'

Frank smiled. The good news made the men relax, so Jasper went to stand beside him. He was making gestures at Rattigan while muttering to Frank, but Frank seemed to wave a dismissive hand at whatever he was saying.

Jasper looked angry enough to react rashly, but Frank forestalled any chance of that when he beckoned for Rattigan to approach.

'Then tell Schneider to bring the wagon into the mine,' he said.

Rattigan sighed. 'I'm afraid I can't do that. Schneider wants you to come to the wagon to discuss terms.'

'There are no terms to discuss. I've already paid for this delivery.'

Rattigan tipped back his hat. Schneider was now only the same distance away from him as Frank was, and if he tried to explain Schneider's plan to Frank, Schneider would hear him and he'd get a bullet in the back for his trouble.

'Even if you have paid, you still need to go over there and talk with him.'

'I don't care what plans you've cooked up with Schneider. You two will never be welcome here again. Lester has got some questions to answer about why he hired you.'

'If that's your decision, I can accept

it, but Schneider's adamant about one thing: those supplies aren't coming into the mine until you speak with him.'

Frank kicked at the ground and then waved at his men to stay back.

'All right. I guess you're giving me no choice but to comply.'

Frank turned to Jasper, who grinned, seemingly pleased to have been proved right that something was amiss.

Frank pointed a finger, presumably giving him an order to stay back with the other men before he, Frank, moved on towards Rattigan. Frank walked past, looking ahead at the wagon, without acknowledging Rattigan, so giving Rattigan no chance to warn him.

Rattigan and Callan slipped in behind him and the three men headed to the mouth of the entrance.

'I wasn't lying to you,' Rattigan called after Frank. 'We're close to working out why men have been going missing, and even why supplies have been stolen. Once this is over, we can — '

'Be quiet. I wasn't lying to you when

I said you're finished at the mine. I no longer want to hear about anything you've uncovered.'

'Does that include the identity of the man we need to question about the disappearances?' Rattigan walked on for five paces, but Frank didn't reply. 'We don't know yet whether what's been happening is deliberate or a series of unfortunate accidents, but the man who does know is an old friend of yours that you haven't seen for a year.'

Frank bunched his shoulders, but he didn't reply and so they walked on towards the wagon.

Schneider and the others were lined up on the driver's seat. When Frank stopped ten paces from the lead horses, the men glanced at each before agreeing that Schneider and Vick would get down.

These men walked forward to stand five paces away from Frank.

'I remember you,' Frank said, pointing at Vick. 'Until a few weeks ago you used to work for me. Then you left. If you have a grievance about your time here, this isn't the way to resolve it.'

'Our grievance is with Jasper, and Jasper works for you,' Vick said.

Frank gestured at them and then turned to point at Rattigan and Callan.

'So all you men are united by your hatred of Jasper.'

Vick smiled while Schneider licked his lips, but neither man looked as if he would rebut the claim. Rattigan moved forward to stand beside Frank.

'Callan and I do hate Jasper, but only for what he did at Ash Valley. They hate him because he stands between them and their chance to gain from this situation.'

Frank shook his head and turned back to Vick.

'What is this situation?' he asked.

'It's simple,' Vick said. 'We have supplies and you have money. In a short while you'll have supplies and we'll have money.'

'Except those are my supplies. I've already paid for them.'

'You paid Benjamin and Lester, and we killed Benjamin. So believe me when I say that if we don't get what we want, we'll leave with the wagon and let you all starve.' Vick licked his lips. 'I reckon within a few days you'll be so hungry you'll be eating each other.'

Frank tipped back his hat to mop his brow, his worried reaction suggesting that their supplies were even lower than he'd admitted and that this taunt might be valid.

'What do you want?'

'We're not greedy men. Double what you paid already will get you the food, and if you don't give us no trouble, that price will hold for the next three deliveries.'

Frank lowered his head for a moment, then raised a hand.

'Give me a moment to consider,' he said.

'Take all the moments you need,' Vick said.

Frank paced to and fro in the way he'd done when he'd rebuked them in his office. When that forced him to look at Rattigan and Callan, he turned away and walked towards one side of the entrance.

Rattigan watched him until he stopped. Then Frank placed a foot on to a rock and raised his hat to mop his brow as he mulled over the offer.

Rattigan turned back to face Schneider, who smirked with confidence, but only briefly. His eyes narrowed and he looked past Rattigan through the mine entrance.

A moment later a great outcry went up. Rattigan swirled round to see Frank dive behind the rock, while inside the mine men hurried to take up positions on either side of the entrance.

Jasper was in the lead and, on the run, several men raised their guns. Then the shooting started.

12

In a sustained burst Jasper's gunmen fired at Schneider's group, but the first volley of slugs flew wide of their targets.

Unfortunately, Rattigan and Callan were standing between the wagon and the mine. As Rattigan knew Jasper would welcome their getting caught in the cross-fire, either accidentally or otherwise, he and Callan did the only thing they could do.

They flung themselves into prone positions and sought to save themselves by using the cover afforded by the gently undulating ground.

For their part Schneider and Vick hunkered down and blasted lead at Jasper's men, while Dempster cringed down on the seat of the wagon and worked off his anger by firing at Frank. His shots were ineffectual as Frank had chosen a good spot to hide, presumably before giving Jasper the order to attack by raising his hat.

Accordingly, Dempster found himself to be an open target for Jasper's men. When gunfire again ripped out from several gunmen most of the shots flew wide, but then Dempster sat up straight and uttered a howl of anguish.

Dempster swayed, then toppled over sideways, a hand clutched to his bloodied chest. He twitched once and then lay still, his demise drew the attention of Schneider, who nudged Vick and pointed at the wagon.

Schneider and Vick loosed off a couple of shots and then made as though to run for the wagon, but a sustained burst of gunfire tore out from behind Rattigan. The slugs peppered the ground between them and the wagon, and after venturing forward for only a few paces, both men backed away and emulated Rattigan and Callan in diving to the ground.

With no clear target to aim at, Jasper's men stayed their fire. After the lull had dragged on for a minute,

Rattigan shuffled round so that he faced the mine.

He raised his head and then ducked down when lead whistled into the ground a foot to his side. During his brief look around he'd seen Jasper's men making their way closer while seeking the available cover along the sides of the entrance.

They were still too far away to deliver accurate shots, but if they continued to advance, in the next few minutes that would change.

Schneider and Vick appeared to accept that they would struggle to prevail as they started snaking along on their bellies towards the wagon. They soon disappeared from sight behind the horses, but Rattigan judged it would still take them another minute to reach the wagon.

As they would then stand a good chance of escaping, Rattigan attracted Callan's attention. He nodded towards the wagon and Callan replied by doing the same.

Then they both raised themselves for

as far as they dared before kicking off from the ground and running for the wagon.

They kept their heads down and covered several paces before gunfire erupted. Lead kicked dirt from the ground to Rattigan's side.

Figuring the shooters would soon get him in their sights, Rattigan dived to the ground. As Callan took his own evasive action by jerking to the side, Rattigan rolled and came up on his feet.

Callan was nearest the wagon. Keeping his head down he sprinted the last few paces and then tried to vault up on to the seat. He came to a halt with one foot on a wheel and the other dangling when he found that Dempster's body was impeding his progress.

As another burst of gunfire blasted, Rattigan hunkered down beside the wagon. With his teeth gritted he accepted he could do nothing to help Callan. Thankfully, he didn't notice any shots coming close, but Callan still wasted valuable moments in dragging the body off the seat.

When Callan vaulted up and moved along the seat, Rattigan swung himself up to sit beside him. While Callan grabbed the reins, Rattigan looked forward at the mine entrance.

Only a few of Jasper's men were visible, but Schneider and Vick had rallied. While they edged closer to the wagon they were peppering a round of shots that was keeping their opponents down.

They were only a few paces away when Vick swung round to look at the wagon. His shocked expression made it plain that he had been unaware that Rattigan and Callan had made a move for the wagon and had already climbed on to it.

Callan cracked the reins and moved the wagon on with a lurch. His action made Vick snarl and swing his gun arm round to aim at them.

Rattigan and Callan both ducked down and Vick's shot ripped into the seat above them. The gunfire attracted

Schneider's attention and he turned to face them.

He was further away and in a position where he could see both men clearly. He blasted off a last shot at the entrance and then took careful aim at them.

Rattigan thrust his head down until his cheek rested on the seat. Then Schneider fired and Callan cried out in pain.

Rattigan shifted round to find his deputy slipping off the seat. He clamped a hand on his shoulder to keep him steady, while with the other hand he held the reins.

The wagon was now moving at a decent pace. Both gunmen blasted off shots that tore into the side of the wagon, but then the wagon moved past them and they were out of Rattigan's sight.

He shoved Callan's hip until his legs and shoulders were pressed against the back of the seat. He could now see that his deputy had been shot in the side, but he was still breathing, so Rattigan concentrated on getting away.

He looked ahead, but before he could see the path the wagon was taking, Schneider came back into sight. He ran along beside the wagon trying to catch hold of the seat so that he could vault up.

Like Callan before him, he had to struggle to find a way up, this time because Callan's sprawling feet were in the way. Then Rattigan urged more speed from the horses and Schneider dropped back.

Rattigan peered ahead. He saw that the wagon was moving towards the mine entrance. Even if Callan hadn't been shot he would still have gone there, but Callan's injury added to his urgency.

He encouraged the horses to hurtle on and within moments the wagon rattled through the entrance. Then it moved on to pass by the first group of advancing men, all of whom either ignored him to concentrate on Schneider and Vick, or turned to watch him with bemusement.

Rattigan hoped his actions were

clear, and even though nobody cheered him on his way, neither did anyone take a shot at him. As his hopes of reaching a place of safety rose he glanced along the side of the wagon.

Schneider and Vick hadn't risked following him into the mine; instead they were scurrying towards the rocks where Frank had holed up. This action was clearly of concern to Jasper's men as they fired at them.

Rattigan didn't see how this situation developed as he reached the clear area beyond the entrance, after which he swung the wagon towards the miners' camp.

He scattered in his wake the miners who had gathered to support Jasper's men. Then he slowed the wagon from its headlong dash, bringing it to a halt beside the camp and a dozen yards from the buildings.

He wasted no time in checking on Callan, who was groaning although he mustered enough energy to look around at their surroundings. Rattigan raised his jacket to find that Callan had only a small patch of blood on his shirt.

He decided to take this as a good sign. With an arm around Callan's shoulders to keep him sitting upright, he manoeuvred him to the edge of the seat. Then he stood on the wheel and looked for a way to get Callan down without hurting him any more.

Miners were hurrying closer, so he beckoned them to hurry up and help him.

'Don't wait for them,' Callan said through gritted teeth. 'I can make it.'

Rattigan nodded and jumped down. Then he held up his arms to support Callan as he came down.

When he landed on the ground Callan stumbled, but then he managed to stand hunched over. Rattigan urged him to move backwards and lean against the side of the wagon. By the time he'd accomplished this the first miners had arrived and formed a line in front of them.

Despite what Rattigan had just done,

they all glared at him.

'Callan needs help,' Rattigan said, gesturing at the nearest man. 'He's been shot.'

The man didn't reply, but everyone muttered angrily to each other. Rattigan repeated his demand; this time one man stepped forward and sneered at him.

'That's what you both deserve after you tried to shoot up Jasper,' he said, his comment drawing nods and grunts of agreement from the others.

'We just rescued the supplies. Schneider Wilson wasn't happy about that and he shot Callan, just like he's trying to shoot Frank now.'

The man opened his mouth and then closed it, clearly struggling to find a retort.

'Jasper will save him,' he said, leaving no doubt as to where his loyalties lay. 'Just like he saved the supplies.'

Rattigan shook his head in exasperation. Then he looked past the miners in the hope that he might find someone who would help Callan. He failed to see anyone who looked at them with any-thing less than disgust and, worse, over by the entrance Jasper was striding into view.

Several of the gunmen were trailing behind him, which suggested that the gunfight had been brought to an end, but Rattigan didn't wait around to find out how it had turned out for Frank or for Schneider and Vick. He told Callan to rest an arm over his shoulder and then walked him away from the wagon.

As the miners edged towards him he headed for the saloon. Nobody made an effort to help him, so they shuffled on while a clamour of voices grew behind them as more miners gathered.

They were fifty paces from the saloon when Jasper's voice rang out, although he was still some distance away and behind the bulk of the miners.

'Stop them getting away,' he shouted. 'They were trying to help those men steal the supplies.'

This claim was so outrageous that Rattigan turned to give a vehement denial, but he faced a line of angry men waving fists, none of whom were looking as if they were prepared to listen to reason. He turned back and urged Callan to move faster.

Callan tried to increase the length of his stride, but he stumbled and Rattigan spent valuable moments getting him standing upright again before they continued on their way. Then rapid footfalls sounded as the miners followed Jasper's instruction.

They had covered half the distance to the saloon when Rattigan saw movement on either side of them as the miners sought to surround them.

'Just a few more paces,' Rattigan said.

'Then what?' Callan said. His voice was barely audible and his step faltered again.

Rattigan didn't have an answer, but shadows spread around them and harsh breathing sounded on all sides, giving him the impression that their pursuers were within moments of swooping down on them. In a sudden decision he gave up helping Callan to walk; instead he moved behind him.

He wrapped his arms around Callan's chest. Then, heedless of the pain he would probably inflict, he swung round to walk backwards to the saloon as quickly as he could while dragging Callan along.

He had been right that the miners had closed in on three sides. Perhaps in acceptance that even when they reached the saloon there was nowhere else for them to go, they only formed a solid wall of men and kept pace with them.

Rattigan continued to drag Callan along. With a glance over his shoulder at the saloon he aligned himself with the entrance and nudged his way in through the batwings. Only one customer was in there, and he was lurking in the shadows with his head down. Then the first miner looked as though he would follow Rattigan in, together with two other men who were close behind him.

Rattigan reckoned that if he didn't stop them coming in the room would fill up rapidly. So with no other choice he lowered Callan to the floor, stepped over him, and thudded a swinging punch into the first man's cheek.

The blow knocked the man backwards and into the two men who were attempting to come in with him. All three men tumbled down outside. Rattigan moved on to the doorway.

'I'm the marshal of the Barren Plains,' he declared, closing the batwings and standing behind them. 'You men will stay out there. The only person I'll allow in is anyone who is prepared to help Callan.'

Rattigan glared around the gathered men. He met as many eyes as he could, seeking to force them to back down purely through his authority.

To his surprise nobody made a move to come in and when the fallen men got to their feet they slipped away and mingled with the crowd. This encouraged more men to back away. Rattigan rolled his shoulders, but before he could congratulate himself on his success, from the corner of his eye he saw the glint of gunmetal.

He glanced that way to see that the customer had intervened. While keeping in the shadows, he had rested a wrist on the top of a batwing and he was now swinging a six-shooter from side to side in a threatening manner.

Rattigan turned to see who it was who had helped him. When his gaze reached the man's face, he couldn't help but gasp.

Woodrow Albright was smiling at him.

'I figured that you needed a friend right now,' Woodrow said.

13

'I'm obliged,' Rattigan said with genuine relief.

He was even more obliged when Woodrow pressed another six-shooter into his hand. Rattigan kept the gun low and out of sight to avoid inflaming the situation.

Nobody made a move to advance on the door, but at the back of the group men spread out as Jasper arrived with several gunmen trailing behind him.

These men struggled to make their way closer, and with everyone pressed together tightly Rattigan judged that Jasper would need another few minutes to reach the saloon. He looked further afield; by the entrance he could just make out Frank.

Frank had gathered men around him and was giving orders. Then those men hurried off to the mine entrance and disappeared from view; their behaviour suggested that Schneider and Vick had escaped and Frank was dispatching a group to track them down.

Frank then turned to the settlement. He appraised the situation before setting off towards them. He wouldn't arrive for several minutes and Jasper was most of the way through the group.

'What are you men waiting for?' Jasper shouted when only three men stood between him and the saloon. 'Get him out of there.'

'Someone's got a gun on us,' someone said.

'And in a moment I'll have ten guns on him.'

Rattigan reckoned that only three gunmen were trailing behind Jasper, but the boast gave everyone heart and they edged forward.

'Everyone stay back,' Rattigan demanded. 'This is your only warning.'

The miners ignored him and continued to edge forward menacingly, making Woodrow utter a squeal of concern and then lower his gun. Rattigan was about to order him to return, but then he noticed that he had bent down to check on Callan.

The removal of the visible gun made Jasper smile and with firm shoves he knocked the last few men aside until he stood clear of the miners.

'I'm not listening to that order,' he said. 'It's time to end this, Rattigan.'

His gaze set on Rattigan, Jasper reached for his gun, his movement slow as he relished in anticipation the moment when he would defeat him. Rattigan didn't move until Jasper drew his gun; then, with the same level of relish, he raised his own weapon above the batwings.

Jasper flinched with surprise before raising his gun arm, but by then Rattigan was already firing. From close range his shot caught Jasper between the eyes, causing his head to snap back.

Jasper toppled into the men standing behind him, sending a ragged row of men stumbling away. Rattigan kept his gun in sight, hoping this would end the confrontation, but with a snarl of anger one of Jasper's men blasted a shot at him from the crowd.

The lead sliced into the top of the batwing on which Rattigan's hand was resting. Rattigan sought out the shooter, but so many men were facing the saloon that he failed to spot him. The miners must have picked up on his reluctance to fire indiscriminately, as they charged forward.

Another shot rang out, this time whistling over Rattigan's head, and then men crowded into the doorway, curtailing further gunfire. Rattigan backed away and turned, to find that Callan was no longer lying on the floor near the door.

He quickly spotted Woodrow dragging Callan around the side of the bar. He wasted no time in following. He joined them as Woodrow reached the door leading to the back rooms in one of which he'd slept the night before.

Rattigan held the door open; by the time Woodrow had slipped through, miners were pouring into the saloon.

'Forget about them,' Woodrow called. 'Just keep going.'

'There's nowhere to go back there,' Rattigan said, although he took Woodrow's advice and hurried through the door.

Then he looked for something to bar the miners' path; finding only a table, he upended it and pressed it up against the door. He judged it would hold the mob off for only a few moments.

Seeing no other means of delaying them for any longer, he followed Woodrow.

There was only one back door in the building, but leaving by that means wouldn't help them. As it gave immediately on to the rock face the only direction they could take would bring them back towards the miners.

Woodrow appeared to be aware of this as he headed for the first door along the corridor, which he kicked open. Rattigan recalled that Frank had slept in this room.

He hurried on to the doorway, hearing, as he slipped inside, the main door rattling as the miners battered against it.

'Shove everything you can against the door,' Woodrow said as he laid Callan down on the floor.

Rattigan lost no time in doing as Woodrow suggested. He slammed the door shut. Then, after shoving a small cupboard and the cot against the door, he looked for anything else he could use.

'Don't worry,' he said. 'We only need to hold out until Frank arrives.'

Woodrow frowned. 'It's by no means certain that Frank will side with you and call everyone off.'

Rattigan finished looking around the room. It was larger than the one he'd slept in but, failing to see anything useful, he tried to press the cupboard and cot closer to the door.

'I know, but it's the only chance we have. Now, help me make this as secure as we can.'

'You do that. I have more important things to do.'

Rattigan swirled round to glare at Woodrow, only to find that he was tapping a foot on the floor. Then, in the space where the cot had stood, a hollow thud sounded.

Woodrow dropped to his knees and tapped around before slipping his fingers into an indentation in the floor. Then he drew up a trapdoor.

'Larry Walker's work?' Rattigan asked with an approving whistle.

'Sure,' Woodrow said, raising a surprised eyebrow. Then he dismissed the matter of how Rattigan knew this and jumped down into the hole he'd revealed, to disappear up to his shoulders. 'This tunnel was dug in the early days and kept open in case of trouble like this. I suggest we use it.'

Rattigan nodded and hurried over to Callan. He took him by his shoulders and dragged him closer to the hole.

'I can make it,' Callan said, so Rattigan left him on the edge of the hole.

Callan swung his legs over the edge.

Then, with Woodrow holding his hips, he lowered himself down.

Rattigan followed. As he was lowering himself a thud sounded in the corridor as the miners broke through the first door. Woodrow reached up and swung the trapdoor down.

Rattigan feared they would be plunged into darkness, but a surprising amount of light still flooded into the tunnel, which stretched away from them. He peered down the tunnel and judged that the light source came from somewhere ahead.

With Woodrow leading and Rattigan at Callan's shoulder in case he needed help again, they moved on.

Shouted orders sounded behind them as the miners explored the back rooms of the saloon, but Rattigan didn't hear anyone try the door suggesting they were reluctant to enter Frank's room. He doubted this would hold them off for long and sure enough, just as the tunnel began to lead upwards, fists pounded on the door.

As they continued climbing the

hammering sounds receded into the distance. If the miners broke into the room, it wouldn't take them long to work out where the fugitives had gone and follow. Then a potential source of confusion presented itself when they emerged into a hollowed-out cave.

Another tunnel led downwards, others led from the sides and two more led upwards. Woodrow took the tunnel that was lit up, but Rattigan judged that if they could cut off that light source, their route wouldn't be obvious to the miners.

As he waited for Callan to slip into the tunnel after Woodrow, Rattigan glanced down the various tunnels, wondering where they all led. He smiled to himself and then followed Callan.

'As these tunnels are Larry Walker's work, I assume one of them leads to the store,' he called after Woodrow.

Woodrow stopped to look down at him. 'There is a tunnel that leads there, but it's not one of these. Now stop wasting time admiring the scenery and follow me.'

Rattigan reckoned this was good advice and he kept quiet as they clambered up for another fifty paces until they came out in another, open, cave. While Woodrow collected a barrier and laid it down over the hole, Rattigan checked on Callan.

Callan's side was now drenched in blood, his exertions clearly having opened up the wound. Rattigan sat him down leaning back against the side of the cave and looked into his eyes until the deputy mustered a weak nod.

Then he helped Woodrow cover the barrier with other lengths of wood that were lying around the cave. There was nothing close at hand that was heavy enough to make it difficult for anyone to get out, but it was by no means certain that without light anyone would find their way to this cave.

When the job was done to Woodrow's satisfaction he hurried out of the cave without comment. Rattigan helped Callan to his feet; this time the deputy didn't refuse his help.

Towering rocks surrounded the cave

and Rattigan could see no way forward, but Woodrow knew where he was going. He worked his way forward, always climbing but never moving too far ahead so that Rattigan could always see where they had to go.

Their progress was slow, but Rattigan heard no signs of a pursuit and he began to think they might get away from the mine. But then Callan stumbled and they stopped as Rattigan struggled to get him back on his feet.

'How much further?' Rattigan called.

'Not far,' Woodrow called over his shoulder. Then he stopped and turned, as if he'd accepted his comment hadn't sounded convincing. 'The going becomes easier soon.'

'And this route takes us out of the mine?'

Woodrow nodded and gestured to them to keep moving. The brief break had given Callan enough strength to set off again, and he moved with even greater ease when Woodrow's promise proved to be correct.

They started working their way downwards. Rocks still blocked Rattigan's view so that he couldn't see where they were going, but he judged that they were getting close to ground level when Woodrow called a halt.

He bade them to wait, then he advanced, disappearing from view after a few paces. Ten minutes later he returned to report that they could move on.

Woodrow leading, they stumbled past two large rocks before emerging on to the plains. Woodrow glanced around before moving to the right.

Then, keeping the higher ground around the mine to one side, he worked his way along. He didn't stray out on to the plains for more than a few yards.

From what they'd seen earlier, Schneider and Vick were probably still at large with Frank's men looking for them, so Rattigan joined him in looking around.

He saw nothing to perturb him and after five minutes, with a knowing wink, Woodrow slipped between two rocks that looked no different to Rattigan from the hundreds of other boulders that littered the base of the higher ground.

Beyond was a surprisingly large area of flat ground, surrounded on all sides by high, vertical rocks.

'Keep to the sides,' Woodrow said. 'Sometimes the sand can be treacherous.'

This revelation made Callan raise his head to smile at Rattigan. At that moment a man stepped into view ahead. He nodded to Woodrow, then beckoned him on.

Woodrow moved on, heeding his own advice to stay close to the rock. Rattigan followed his path, and when they reached the man Rattigan saw that other people had gathered in an alcove in the rock that protected them from view from most sides.

Six men were here: he recognized only one of them. This man stepped forward.

'I'm pleased to meet you, again,' the man said.

'And we're pleased to meet you again, Larry Walker,' Rattigan replied.

'You've clearly been doing some thinking, but perhaps not enough.' The man smiled. 'I'm Percival Walker, Larry's brother.'

14

'So what happened to Larry?' Rattigan asked when he'd helped Callan to sit down.

Percival directed a bearded man to help Callan and then sighed.

'I'm afraid he died last year, just like everyone reckons he did,' he said. 'He tried to walk out of the Barren Plains and, despite being the only man who might have been able to do that, he failed.'

Rattigan noted that the bearded man examined Callan's wound in a matter-of-fact manner that suggested he had medical knowledge, so he moved aside to give him room to work.

'So what are you doing here?' he asked.

'I'm looking for his body.'

Rattigan nodded. 'You reckon he died when he fell into a sinkhole. So you've been emptying them out one at a time and you'll keep going until you find the one that claimed his life.'

Percival raised an eyebrow in surprise. 'Clearly I rescued a perceptive man.'

'And clearly you're a devoted brother to search for him for so long.'

Percival rocked his head from side to side and then smiled.

'I did care for my brother.' He withdrew a small bag from his pocket and emptied its contents on to his palm. 'But these have spurred on my search even more.'

At first Rattigan couldn't see what Percival was showing him, but when the men who had gathered in the clearing leaned forward expectantly, he narrowed his eyes. Still, he could only just make out what looked like small fragments of glass, but then one of the pieces caught a beam of light and sparkled enticingly.

'Jewels?'

'Diamonds.'

'And they were dug up at the mine?'

'Near to the mine, but I don't know where exactly Larry found them.'

With extreme care Percival tipped the diamonds back into the bag; several men sighed as they disappeared from view. The obvious interest everyone showed made Rattigan frown and he pieced together the situation as he moved on to see how Callan was faring.

The bearded man had now raised Callan's shirt and was prodding around the wound. Callan was leaning back with a pained grimace on his face.

'He says the bullet scraped a furrow,' Callan said. 'When he's cleaned it out, I'll be fine.'

On hearing this good news Rattigan turned back to Percival.

'Larry used his expert knowledge to find those diamonds,' he said, 'but he kept that knowledge to himself so that he didn't have to share his discovery with Frank. Now you're left floundering in his wake.'

'That's right, but don't judge Larry harshly. Frank would have done the same to him if he'd found the diamonds first.'

'I'm not judging nobody.' Rattigan looked around the group. 'But I reckon you recruited others to aid your search, and they all feigned their deaths to make it look as if they'd disappeared without trace.'

Percival nodded. 'The only man from Bleak Point who has ever truly disappeared never to be seen again is Larry. I had tried to keep my search a secret, but sneaking into the mine to get supplies eventually caught someone's attention. Then, as more people found out about my quest, it's become even harder to keep the secret and so yet more people have joined me.'

'Because the prize if you can find the place where Larry dug up those diamonds is a more enticing option than having to deal with Jasper Minx?'

'It is. The contents of this bag is more than any miner could hope to earn in ten lifetimes, but I've long since given up on finding the place. Now, all I want is to find the sinkhole that swallowed up my brother.' Percival smiled. 'Along with the diamond that was in his pocket at the time.'

'I assume that diamond is bigger than the ones you showed me?'

'Sure. Larry sent me the small ones for safekeeping. His letter said he'd found one a hundred times larger and he was bringing it with him. He never arrived.' Percival frowned and moved on to the mouth of the alcove. 'His body, and that diamond, is lying somewhere in the Barren Plains.'

Rattigan joined him. 'If Larry was swallowed up by the sand, it could take a lifetime to find the right sinkhole.'

'I know. That's why I've offered everyone who has joined me an equal share in the diamond.' He pointed at the sand ahead. 'I've learnt plenty about this terrain and I believe another hole is over there. We'll start work on it later. If we're lucky, our quest ends here. If not, we'll move on to the next one.'

Rattigan turned back to consider the

group. Most of them were now chatting with Woodrow or casting concerned glances at the newcomers; the brief snippets of conversation that he overheard enabled him to identify some of them.

Burl Jenkins, who had been the first of the six men to have gone missing recently, was here, along with the man who had guarded the supplies and Woodrow's friend Jefford. Rattigan assumed the other two men who were known to have disappeared were also here.

'Frank Holmes appointed me as marshal of the Barren Plains,' Rattigan said, raising his voice to address the group. 'Our relationship has soured and even if we could sort that out, his miners will kill me if I set foot in the mine again. So I won't tell anyone what I've learnt here.'

His declaration made a few men nod, but others still regarded him with stern expressions.

'We're obliged to hear that,' Woodrow said.

He still sounded cautious and, after a

moment's thought about what was worrying them, Rattigan smiled.

'And you all need to know that I have no interest in joining you to claim another share in the missing diamond.'

This time his declaration made everyone smile and, his having correctly identified the problem, the group settled down. Percival moved over to watch as Callan's injury was cleaned up, while Woodrow joined Rattigan.

'All these extra people arriving recently has made the original recruits nervous,' Woodrow said. 'They made it clear that after me no more would be accepted, but your explanation put their minds at rest and it proves I was right to help you.'

'I'm grateful for what you did.' Rattigan sighed. 'And I guess I ought to forgive you for lying about Jasper's intentions in Ash Valley.'

'I didn't lie. He duped me as much as he duped . . . ' Woodrow shrugged. 'But I guess that doesn't matter none now that Jasper's dead.'

'I guess it doesn't.' Rattigan looked around the alcove and then up to the high rocks that surrounded the mine. 'Callan and I have delivered the supplies. We've solved the mystery of the disappearing people and we've made Jasper pay. There's only one thing left for us to do out here now.'

'Which is?'

Woodrow looked at him oddly, confirming that he couldn't have seen everything that had gone on prior to rescuing him. Rattigan would have been content to leave things that way, but Schneider and Vick would be looking for somewhere to hole up close to the mine, while Frank's men would be searching for them.

'Come on,' he said. 'We need to keep lookout. Aside from the possibility of the miners finding us, two men are on the loose and looking for a place to hide.'

Woodrow was the only other man in the group who was armed, so he accompanied Rattigan as he slipped out of the alcove. They made their way to the entrance to the sandy area, ensuring they stayed close to the edge.

Rattigan directed Woodrow to take one side of the entrance while he took the other. His order made Woodrow smile.

'After everything that happened between us, I never thought I'd get to take your orders,' he said.

'Believe me, if Callan was fit, I wouldn't be doing it now.'

Woodrow chuckled. 'I'll settle for that.'

He moved to the side of the entrance to peer at the plains beyond. Then he flinched and jerked his head back. A gunshot rang out.

Woodrow staggered backwards a pace. Then he toppled over on to his back, revealing a red hole in the centre of his chest.

15

Rattigan trained his gun on the side of the entrance where Woodrow had been shot while he edged sideways towards the other side.

Slowly the terrain beyond came into view. Woodrow had been shot at short range and Rattigan figured that the shooter had been standing just round the corner from the entrance, which meant that in a few more paces he would be able to see him.

Sure enough, after two more paces, a foot and a lower leg came into view followed by a hand. The man must have realized his discovery was imminent, as with a sudden movement he swung out to face Rattigan, training his gun round to aim at him.

With only a moment to act Rattigan saw that he was facing Vick; he fired low, catching him in the lower chest.

Vick wasted a shot into the ground as he stumbled a pace, but a second shot higher on the chest downed him.

Rattigan swung round as he searched for Schneider. He didn't see him, but Percival called out from the alcove.

'Watch out!' he shouted.

Rattigan couldn't see what had alerted Percival, but he backed away, which helped to limit the impact when Schneider leapt down from a high rock above him. Schneider still caught him around the shoulders and both men went down. Rattigan landed on his back and with Schneider sprawled on top of him.

Rattigan shook his head to gather his senses while Schneider raised himself. Then, straddling Rattigan's chest, Schneider batted the gun from his hand, sending it hurtling away.

Schneider settled his weight down on him and swung his own gun into view. Rattigan didn't give him time to aim and with an upward thrust of his hips he sought to buck Schneider away.

Schneider rocked to one side before steadying himself. Rattigan took advantage of Schneider's brief period of imbalance to sit up and lunge for his gun arm.

He closed a hand around Schneider's wrist, then thrust the hand high and away from him. His action made Schneider snarl and, with his other hand opened flat, Schneider delivered a blow to the underside of Rattigan's jaw that rocked his head back. Rattigan still kept hold of Schneider's wrist.

Schneider repeated the blow and when that failed to loosen Rattigan's tight grip, he lunged forward. His weight made Rattigan rock backwards, but as he fell he twisted and thrust up with a hip.

This time he dislodged Schneider, who fell to the side. Their limbs being entangled, Rattigan ended up falling with him and the two men rolled over each other.

Schneider struggled and that made them roll again. The thought hit Rattigan that they were moving into the open ground that Percival had warned him to avoid, so he sought to roll the other way.

His action only encouraged Schneider to redouble his efforts to make them continue moving along their original course. They rolled over each other one more time before they came to rest lying on their sides facing each other.

Each man strained to bring the gun down and aim it at the other, but their combined efforts only made the gun jerk around wildly. The gun swung back and forth twice; then Schneider lost his grip of the weapon and it went flying away.

Schneider twisted to watch the gun's progress until it flopped down on the ground three yards away. Rattigan judged that his own gun had been hurled into this area, but it was no longer visible; he supposed that the sand could have swallowed it up.

Schneider wouldn't know this and he battered at Rattigan with fists and elbows as he tried to free himself.

Percival and the other men had emerged from the alcove to watch the fight, but they were making no effort to intervene; possibly they were aware that the sinkhole could be close by.

As Rattigan was reluctant to move towards the gun, Schneider's berserk actions enabled him to tear himself free. Then, with a cry of triumph, he leapt towards the gun.

Rattigan grabbed Schneider's thigh, halting him and Schneider flopped down to the ground with his outstretched hand a foot from the gun.

'Do something,' Rattigan called to Percival.

'There's nothing we can do,' Percival called back.

'Woodrow had a gun.'

Percival swirled round to look to the entrance and then set off running, but this added urgency to Schneider's attempts to reach the gun. He dragged himself forward, his hand clawing ever closer to the weapon.

Rattigan tugged, trying to draw him

back, but Schneider moved inexorably onwards. Then, making a sudden decision, he rolled up on to his haunches and dived for the gun. He landed beside Schneider and the tip of a finger brushed the barrel.

Then the gun disappeared into the sand.

Both men looked at the space where the gun had been. Then a rumble sounded below them and the ground no longer felt solid.

Rattigan's elbows disappeared into sand that now had less consistency than mud.

As Schneider's arms slipped down into the sand, Schneider stared at him with a wide-eyed look of horror on his face. Rattigan ignored him as he concentrated on trying to escape from the sand trap.

He kicked back with his legs, but they had already slipped into the sand. When he pushed down with his arms he couldn't gain any purchase and he flopped back down.

Then Schneider thrust out a hand and slammed it down on the back of his head, shoving his face into the sand.

With his eyes and mouth clamped tightly shut, Rattigan struggled, but he couldn't raise his head; he had the feeling he was just burying himself deeper into the sand.

Acting blindly he dragged his arms up and reached out until his hand clamped on Schneider's shoulder. Then he walked his hand along until he could wrap it around the man's neck.

He pressed in but, with his face beneath the sand, he couldn't tell if he was having an effect until he felt Schneider try to drag himself away. That had the fortunate result of drawing Rattigan's head up and in a burst of showering sand his face emerged.

He shook the sand from his eyes and brought his other hand round to clamp it around Schneider's throat. His movement brought his upper body out of the sand, but his legs and lower body were firmly encased.

He grinned when he found that his head was higher up than Schneider's was. He pressed down until Schneider's body was no longer visible below the shoulders.

'You left me to face the dangers of the Barren Plains,' Rattigan said. 'And now you're learning about those dangers the hard way.'

Schneider tried to retort, but he could manage only a reedy snarl. Then the pressure on his neck forced his chin and then his mouth below the ground.

In moments the rest of his face disappeared from view until only his hat was resting on the surface.

Then the hat slipped down, too. One of Schneider's hands emerged from the sand and it brushed Rattigan's arm, but he failed to gain a grip.

By the time the hand had slipped away Rattigan could no longer keep hold of Schneider's neck, but he figured that that was no longer important. He wriggled forward and found, to his delight, that his feet moved. Then he hit

Schneider's body.

A pointed object brushed his calf, possibly one of Schneider's fingertips. Then a tightness wrapped around his ankle giving him the impression that Schneider was still alive and trying to tug him down.

He figured Schneider would have only limited strength so he reached down to his leg and tried to sweep him away.

His fingers touched a hard surface. It felt like Schneider's bony forehead and he pushed it, feeling something come away in his hand. Then he kicked out with his feet.

Schneider moved until he was beneath Rattigan's feet. As Rattigan figured that he must now be standing on Schneider's sinking body, he shoved down.

With a cry of triumph he rose up and out of the sand. His hands broke free of the surface, showing him that the object that had come away in his hand was Schneider's hat.

His relief was short-lived as he then started sinking again. Within moments the sand rose up above his stomach.

'Don't struggle any more,' Percival called from over by the entrance as he slipped Woodrow's gun into his belt. 'That'll just make you sink faster.'

Rattigan took a deep breath and did as Percival suggested, but the sand continued to rise up his chest, albeit at a slower rate.

'I'm trying to stay still,' he said. 'But that just makes me sink, too.'

Percival hurried over to stand closer to Rattigan.

'It will, but it'll give us more time to get you out of there.'

'I'm obliged, but whatever you're planning on doing, do it quickly.' Rattigan looked at Percival, who didn't move, and then at the others, who had emerged from the alcove and were looking at him with worried expressions. 'How do you usually get people out?'

'We've never had to do it before.' Percival shrugged. 'But I guess there's a first time for everything.'

Percival looked at the others, but he

received only blank stares. He edged towards Rattigan with a hand thrust out, but Rattigan could see that he wouldn't be able to get close enough to help him without endangering himself.

Then, from the alcove, Callan emerged. He walked gingerly and he was no longer wearing his shirt and jacket and his bandaged chest was revealed.

Rattigan watched him, hoping his deputy might come up with a good idea; then he saw that he'd already had one. The shirt and jacket were draped over one arm and he'd tied the ends of the sleeves together with a large, tight knot.

Grim determination tightening his jaw, he walked on until he was level with Percival. Then, clutching hold of a sleeve, he swung round to hurl the garments towards Rattigan.

The shirt unfolded before it reached Rattigan's head and the jacket slapped him in the face.

Rattigan lost no time in grabbing hold of the jacket. He flashed a grateful smile at Callan, but Callan's effort in launching the garments had made him drop to his knees.

He looked to be in no state to continue with his rescue plan, but he didn't need to continue, as Percival rushed over and took hold of the sleeve. While the bearded man hurried forward to help Callan move away, Burl joined Percival.

With two men holding one end of the tied garments, Rattigan moved a hand along the jacket and, when the knot held, he tried to drag himself forward. At first he moved for only a few inches, but at least he was no longer sinking.

When it becoming clear that the garments could take the strain, Percival and Burl moved backwards.

For a moment Rattigan didn't move as the sand held him in a tight embrace making it feel as if they would yank his arms from their sockets, but he held on.

Then, in a rush, he surged forward and he was dragged along the sand. Percival and Burl kept walking backwards until their backs were against the rock face.

Only then did Rattigan feel confident enough that he'd escaped from the sinkhole to stand up.

He nodded his thanks to Callan, then to Percival and Burl before he turned back to face the sand trap that had nearly claimed his life.

The area was still now, the ground having formed a depression similar to the other ones he'd seen across the plains. With an amused smile he noted that he had kept hold of Schneider's hat, the only hint that this man had ever been here.

He shivered and tossed the hat to the ground. Then he moved on to help Callan walk back into the alcove.

16

Rattigan helped Callan to sit down, then he turned to Percival.

'We all need to move on and find somewhere else to hole up,' he said.

'We'll stay here,' Percival said. 'We've yet to explore the sinkhole that you were determined to get a look at first, and we won't leave until we have.'

Rattigan shook his head. 'That brief exchange of gunfire is sure to attract attention.'

'It will, but if they do come here there'll be nothing for them to see.'

Percival pointed past Rattigan. When he turned round he saw two men dragging Woodrow's body into the alcove. Then they hurried away and returned with Vick's body held by the ankles and shoulders.

They took the body a few paces into the sandy area. They stood where

Percival and Burl had stood when they rescued him. Then, without ceremony, they hurled the body as far as they could.

The body hit the ground and lay on its side for a few moments. Then sand began to fill in around it and slowly it slipped down.

Rattigan watched until he could no longer see Vick's form. As had happened with Schneider, after a few minutes the sand spread out to form a smooth area, as if nothing had ever been there.

Then they all slipped back into the alcove where they waited in the shadows with their backs pressed to the rock face.

Rattigan stayed close to the mouth of the alcove with his gun drawn; he judged that a half-hour had passed when he heard voices approaching.

The men were shouting to each other, making it sound as if they were carrying out a search. The voices grew louder and Rattigan reckoned one man called out from only a few yards beyond the entrance to the sandy area.

Then the man moved on and presently the voices faded into the distance.

'I guess you were right that this is as good a hiding-place as any,' Rattigan said, turning to Percival. 'So what will you do now?'

'We'll wait until tomorrow before we begin work on exploring this sinkhole.' Percival glanced at the wounded Callan. 'If you don't want to return to the mine, you're welcome to stay with us until Callan is fit enough to attempt to get out of here.'

'Could we do that afoot?'

'I've left food and water all over the Barren Plains, so with my guidance you should reach Redemption.'

Rattigan nodded and moved over to hunker down beside Callan, who shuffled up to sit upright and then winced in pain.

'I'll need at least a week before I try walking across the plains again,' he said through gritted teeth.

'I agree, and I guess you've answered

my other question.'

Callan looked thoughtful for a moment, then frowned.

'If you're talking about whether or not we should return to the mine, I don't reckon we can even consider it. We could deal with the miners hating us, but we've lost Frank's confidence.'

'You're right that it would be madness to return,' Rattigan mused, rubbing his jaw.

Callan smiled. 'I can tell from your tone that you're still considering it.'

Rattigan tipped back his hat. 'I guess I've grown bored with always moving on.'

'I know what you mean. With Jasper and Schneider dealt with, it'd be good to stop running.' Callan sighed. 'And I was enjoying being a deputy marshal again.'

'And I was enjoying being a . . . ' Rattigan trailed off, a strange thought coming to him now that the fraught situation was over.

He thought back to the desperate

moments when he'd feared that the sand would claim his life. Even after his opponent had sunk beneath the surface, what he had thought was that a dying Schneider had tried to drag him under, but maybe he'd been mistaken.

He looked at Schneider's hat that he'd tossed aside. The sight made him smile.

'What have you just thought of?' Callan said.

Rattigan patted Callan's shoulder and stood up to face Percival.

'Perhaps there's another way I could continue being the marshal of the Barren Plains,' he said. 'This time, I can do it in all ways.'

Percival furrowed his brow, but when Rattigan continued to look at him he gave a warm smile.

'I guess we have been lucky that so far we've been found only by the occasional man,' he said. 'With so many of us now searching for Larry, I reckon we would welcome having someone to guard us and our interests, and maybe, one day soon, to keep my brother's diamond safe.'

Rattigan nodded and then went over to pick up the discarded hat. He returned and held it out.

'In that case, I reckon my first duty should be to give you this.'

Percival shrugged. 'I don't want that old thing. Just toss it out there and it can join Schneider's body.'

Rattigan shook his head and then raised the hat. Percival could see that it had rotted so badly it was barely holding together.

'I don't reckon I should do that because either Schneider was wearing a very old and threadbare hat, or this is someone else's hat.'

The sight made Callan whistle under his breath while Percival's mouth fell open in shock. Then, with a shaking hand, Percival took the hat from Rattigan.

'Larry's?' he queried.

'This hat proves that someone other than Schneider and Vick is lying under the sand over there, and you told me that Larry is the only man ever to have disappeared without trace in the Barren Plains.'

Percival whooped with delight and then shook Rattigan's hand.

'That sure is some mighty fine reasoning.'

Rattigan smiled. 'More important, that's some mighty fine reasoning from the marshal of the Barren Plains.'

LEGEND OF THE DEAD
MEN'S GOLD
BULLET CATCH SHOWDOWN
ALL MUST DIE
THE MYSTERY OF SILVER FALLS
THE MAN WHO TAMED LONE PINE
INCIDENT AT PEGASUS HEIGHTS
DEVINE'S MISSION

We do hope that you have enjoyed reading this large print book.

Did you know that all of our titles are available for purchase?

We publish a wide range of high quality large print books including:
Romances, Mysteries, Classics
General Fiction
Non Fiction and Westerns

Special interest titles available in large print are:
The Little Oxford Dictionary
Music Book, Song Book
Hymn Book, Service Book

Also available from us courtesy of Oxford University Press:
Young Readers' Dictionary
(large print edition)
Young Readers' Thesaurus
(large print edition)

For further information or a free brochure, please contact us at:
Ulverscroft Large Print Books Ltd.,
The Green, Bradgate Road, Anstey,
Leicester, LE7 7FU, England.
Tel: (00 44) **0116 236 4325**
Fax: (00 44) **0116 234 0205**